SAX

A SAVAGE KINGS MC NOVEL

LANE HART

D.B. WEST

COPYRIGHT

Edited by Angela Snyder

Cover by Marianne Nowicki of www.PremadeEbookCoverShop.com

WARNING: THIS BOOK IS NOT SUITABLE FOR ANYONE UNDER 18. PLEASE NOTE THAT IT CONTAINS VIOLENT SCENES THAT MAY BE A TRIGGER FOR INDIVIDUALS WHO HAVE BEEN IN SIMILAR SITUATIONS.

SYNOPSIS

I never thought I would be stupid enough to make a deal with the devil, but here I am doing just that.

It's not like he really gave me a choice. I have to give the Governor what he wants, or he's going to throw all of my Savage Kings MC brothers into prison for decades.

And what exactly does Governor Satan need from me? That's the real kicker because he's insisting that I...date his daughter. No, not just date her. He wants me to convince Isobel to stop spiraling out of control before she ends up dead, or worse - ruin her father's chance at getting re-elected.

I have no clue why his beautiful wild child is partying her way through life, crossing off items on a mile-long bucket list, and I don't really care. Somehow, someway, I have to convince her to put down roots and go back to being the picture-perfect good girl her father raised.

As if I'm not in deep enough, I've never wanted anyone more than the free-spirit who refuses to spend her short life standing in one place for too long. Too bad Isobel is going to hate my guts when she finds out I'm the asshole who has to lock her back up in a cage.

And if I fail to do so, well, there won't be an orange jumpsuit waiting for me. I'll never make it to prison because the Governor dug up all my dirt that I thought I had carefully buried.

If he tells the Kings that I started prospecting with them as a DEA rat ten years ago, they'll never forgive me.

How could they when I still haven't forgiven myself?

PROLOGUE

Sax

Twelve years ago...

"Hi, Mrs. Neil. This is Sax. Is April there?" I ask when her mother answers the phone.

"Sax?" Mrs. Neil replies with a hitch in her voice. "Oh, Saxon, I'm so sorry. Of course you haven't heard," she trails off as she begins to sob.

An incredible pressure builds in my chest as someone else takes the phone and the crying grows more distant. "Saxon?" a male voice I recognize as April's father says.

"Mr. Neil? Yeah, this is Sax. I didn't hear from April yesterday over Valentine's Day, and I just wanted to call and check in on her. I didn't want to be pushy; I know we agreed to see other people while I'm out here at school, but..."

"Saxon, listen," Mr. Neil interrupts me. "April...April passed away last night. Her mother and I are making arrangements for her memorial, once her autopsy..." his voice trails off in a harsh sob as I slowly lower myself to the foot of the twin bed in my dorm, beyond stunned.

Did he just say...he just said April passed away? That's why she hasn't returned my calls?

"Oh my God," I gasp. "I-I'm so sorry, sir. Wha-what happened?" My voice breaks as tears flood my eyes, and a hot wave of anguish chokes my throat.

"We're not entirely sure yet," Mr. Neil replies after a few moments. "The police showed up here last night and told us that they were called out to some bar...where they found April. The doctors are saying it was an overdose, but we just don't know." He pauses to blow his nose while I let all of that information sink in. "Saxon, if you'll excuse me, I know how close you and April were. I'll let you know as soon as we find out more. For now, I-I need to go, son."

"Of course, sir," I manage to squeak out. I hear the line disconnect just before a hitching sob rips through me, completely incapacitating me. My lungs must have shrunken in my chest, refusing to expand while my heart crumbles around them.

How could April possibly be dead? She and I were good together for two years until last fall when I got accepted to the University of North Carolina at Chapel Hill on a football scholarship. It was only a few hours away, but she had convinced me we should try to see other people until she graduated and could join me. I had agreed, not wanting to pressure her, but had given her a promise ring, which she always wore when I was home visiting. We were planning to have a future together some day...

I knew she had been on some dates with other guys, just like I had hung out with a few other women. I had never known her to do any sort of drugs, though, and had no idea how she could have suffered an overdose.

When I can finally breathe normally again, I throw a few things into my backpack and grab my helmet, determined to ride my old Honda Magna bike all the way back to Emerald Isle tonight.

THE NEXT FEW days pass in a hazy blur of tears intermixed with periods of the most horrifying loneliness I had ever known. April's parents were finally able to get more details about her death, which they shared with me when they called to tell me about her memorial.

She died on the floor of some shithole biker bar called the Savage Asylum, run by a group of local trailer trash that called themselves the Savage Kings. She had died after ingesting some sort of tainted methamphetamine, which the bikers had no doubt supplied her. The police made some unrelated arrests for the drugs, but *nothing*, not a damn thing, has been done about April's death!

I've been so wracked with grief leading up to her memorial that I haven't yet had time to get angry. That all changed during the course of the viewing at the funeral home.

"What the hell are *they* doing here?" I growl at my friend Tony. Tony and I had played football together in high school and graduated together. April's memorial is the first time I've seen him since leaving town.

"Who are you talking about, man?" Tony asks me to clarify.

I jerk my head over towards her silver casket where three men in dark jeans and button up shirts, wearing leather vests, are standing over April. The back of two of the vests are emblazoned with the logo of those goddamned bikers, the Savage Kings.

"Oh, you don't remember him?" Tony asks. "That skinny guy in the prospect vest is Chase Fury. I don't know who the military dudes with him are, though. I haven't seen them around before."

"April died inside their fucking club from drugs they probably gave her. I ought to go over there and beat the shit out of those bastards right now!"

"Dude, Sax, that's a really bad idea," Tony says as he puts a hand on my arm. "Those guys would kill you. Look man," he continues as I shrugged his hand off of me, "I didn't want to lay a bunch of shit on you right now, but April...man, she changed after you left. I get why you're pissed at those guys, but you have to understand, your girl was running around and getting into all kinds of shit."

"What are you talking about? What kind of shit?" I demand, turning back to Tony.

"I'm not here to talk trash on a dead girl," Tony defers softly, raising his hands to pacify me. "I'm just saying that it ain't like those dudes held a pipe to her lips, you know?"

"You're not helping, man," I say on a sigh as I rub my swollen eyes. "I shouldn't have left town. If I had just...if I had just put off college for another year and stayed around for her, she would still be alive."

"Aw, man, you can't know that," Tony starts to say before I interrupt.

"I do know that! This shit wouldn't have happened if I had been here for her. But it did happen. I can't make it right, but I can promise April and her family this: I'm going to get back at those bastards. I'm going to show everyone what they are, and what they did to her. They walk around this town calling themselves fucking 'Kings'. When I'm done with them, people will remember them for the scum they truly are."

CHAPTER ONE

Sax

Present day...

I've never been tortured, but I'm pretty sure nothing could be worse than having an angry cat slice its razor blade claws down your bare chest while you're sleeping.

"What in the ever-loving fuck, Willy!" I yell as I jackknife into a sitting position to assess the damage he just did to my sternum. The little shit has already disappeared when I lift my chain necklace to see if his claws went deep enough to make me bleed.

Thanks to the sunlight streaming in through the port windows, I watch as two sets of red streaks slowly appear on my skin, burning like hellfire.

"Now I know exactly how you lost your eyeball," I grumble to myself.

"W-what?" the naked brunette curled up beside me asks groggily without opening her eyes.

"Nothing. Go back to–" I start to tell her to go back to sleep when I finally hear what obviously sent the evil pussy running for his life.

Barking dogs.

A whole pack of them judging by the chorus growing louder every second.

My boat isn't out to sea, but I am docked at the marina. I have no idea why someone would have a bunch of dogs out here so early in the morning.

"DEA! Come out slowly with your hands behind your head!"

Son of a motherfucking whore.

"Oh shit!" my companion says when she scrambles out of the bed and ducks down beside the mattress.

Are the feds actually coming after the Savage Kings for a few pounds of marijuana? Okay, fine, maybe I've hauled more than a few pounds of weed along with a few large, military-grade firearms. The exact weight of the plants would probably be closer to tons by now. Still, the shit's been legalized in about a dozen states, so it doesn't really make sense why they would give a shit.

I would call the guys to give them a heads-up except my cheap flip cell phone loses signal as soon as you drive into the gates of the marina. Guess the Kings are shit out of luck until I'm given my one phone call in jail. I just hope I don't see them all sitting in lockup first.

Since I don't want the fed assholes barging down here into the galley where some newbie with his finger on the trigger can easily blow my head off along with my not too bright guest's, I quickly grab a white wrinkled Savage Kings t-shirt from the floor to throw over my head, then pull on a worn pair of jeans over my boxer briefs.

"Get up and put some clothes on!" I tell last night's distraction, unable to remember her name at the moment. I'm pretty sure it starts with an L. Maybe. Not that it matters because I won't be sleeping with her again. First of all, it's impossible for my heart to get severed again if I stick to my strict one-night stand only policy; and secondly, if the feds have me surrounded, then I'm guessing my nights may not be free for a few months, or hell, *years*.

Thankfully, the girl listens to me. She quickly redresses in her slutty red halter dress that she was wearing last night when I picked her up at the bar.

"Keep your hands where they can see them, don't make any sudden movements, and just do whatever they say, okay?" I tell her in a rush, and her brown rat's nest bobs, giving me a nod of understanding. "Let's go."

Even though the booming voice told me to come up with my hands on my head, I hold them straight up in the air, palms empty so they can be sure I'm not armed just before my head clears the deck.

Standing in front of my boat on the wooden dock are four guys in suits with their handguns pointed in our direction and another four in black utility uniforms. Each of those men are holding a dog leash that's threatening to snap thanks to the surging, growling, barking German Shepherds on each of the ends.

"Oh shit, oh shit, oh shit," my latest regret is chanting over and over from behind me. I don't even swivel my neck around to see if she's following my orders, afraid to make any sudden movements.

"What's going on?" I shout over the noise.

"Saxon Cole, you're under arrest!" one of the gun-toting dickheads yells loud enough to be heard over the ear-splitting raucous. "We also have a warrant to search your boat!" Slipping his gun into his shoulder holster, he pulls out a folded sheet of paper from the inside of his suit jacket.

"Let her off the boat," I say with a tip of my head behind me. "She just met me last night and doesn't know anything."

With a nod, the fed holding the papers waves the girl over to the dock; and she scurries off my boat and huddles in his arms. Then she has the nerve to glare at me like I'm now some kind of villain. Hell, she was the one who put *my* hand between her bare legs in the bar last night and asked if I wanted to get out of there.

"So what the fuck am I accused of doing?" I bellow at the fed as I lower my hands to the back of my head as he originally requested.

"Somebody cuff him and then let the dogs search," I hear him order, ignoring my question. "No surprise they've already caught the scent of drugs."

"I'll save you boys some time," I reply. "There are no drugs on my boat. But there *is* a half-feral cat in the galley. He's a mean little thunder cunt who will gladly claw your dogs' eyeballs out," I warn the idiots because it would be a mistake if they corner the feisty feline.

As if he answers to the vulgar name, Willy comes barreling up the stairs beside me, skidding as his claws attempt to dig into the slick deck floor. The barking goes from annoying to deafening with his sudden appearance. As if fearing for his life, Willy scrambles up onto the side of the boat and then launches himself through the air and onto the vacant yacht sitting next to my boat.

The drug dogs are then tugging their handlers in the direction of the feline.

I consider taking advantage of the distraction, trying to make a run for the control room just around the corner to start up the engine. But if these fuckers shoot up my boat, I won't get very far before it sinks. And if they shoot *me*, well, I doubt anyone else would adopt Willy once I was gone. God help them if they tried.

Deciding there was really no reason to attempt to flee, I simply say, "Told you so," to the guy I assume is in charge when another one steps onto the boat with me and pulls out a pair of handcuffs.

"You have the right to remain silent," he starts, reading me my Miranda rights. I'm pretty sure this means I'm still fucked, even though they won't find shit during their search.

~

I'M NOT sure how long the government pricks keep me waiting in a cement dungeon with nothing but a cot harder than a boulder and a foul-smelling toilet, but I'm guessing it's around eight to ten hours, judging by my stomach.

The first few hours it growled, hungry for something to eat while I waited for someone, anyone, to come tell me what the hell I'm in here for. While I assume it's drug related charges because they're the Drug Enforcement Agency, they need some sort of proof of illegal activity. For the life of me, I can't figure out what evidence or witnesses they may have.

My mind continues to race with possibilities while my stomach goes from an inconvenient hunger to a constant, gnawing ache. Forget my six-pack of abs, my abdomen is beginning to look more like one giant sinkhole.

Enough is enough!

Getting up from the rock-hard bed, I finally go over and bang my fists on the heavy metal door that only has a tiny sliver of a window. If I stand on my toes of my boots, I can almost see out of it. Almost. All I'm able to make out from this angle is the lights in the ceiling.

"Yo! Did you fuckers forget I'm in here? I want my goddamn phone call!" I roar at the top of my lungs. "Hello! Anyone? You have to fucking feed me and shit! I have rights!"

I pause in my shouting to put my ear to the door and listen for the sound of footsteps or other prisoners, anything.

Nothing. Not a peep. It's like I'm the only person in this entire hellhole, which is good for the other Kings but really sucks for me.

"Dammit!" I exclaim with one last slam of my fist on the door before I trudge back over to the cot and lay down.

I wonder how much time I'm looking at in a shithole like this. Five years in prison, same as Ian? It could be ten years or more for racketeering if they're trying to bring down the club. Fuck, I could even spend the rest of my life in four concrete walls if they somehow found out about the Russian murders. But if it is about the Russians, where the hell is everyone else?

The not knowing is worse than just having them tell me how deep the shit is so I can start preparing myself. But for now, all I can do is wait and think the worst.

CHAPTER TWO

Sax

Hours, maybe days later, after I've fallen asleep, having succumbed to the exhaustion and hunger even though the bright as fuck lights in the dungeon never go out, I startle awake at the sound of a door slamming in the distance. When I sit up, my heart races in my chest with hope that I'll finally get some fucking answers.

My eyes nearly water when I hear keys jingling before the thick cell door swings out, revealing a lean man in a gray, three-piece suit with thick, dark hair that is either a damn good toupee or professionally styled. All I know is that he's definitely not a fed. They can't afford to dress like him. There are several agents standing guard behind him, though.

Also, the front man looks vaguely familiar...

"Who the hell are you?" I ask when I get to my feet. My throat is dry and scratching thanks to the dehydration.

He smiles to show all of his perfect, white teeth while his fingers grip either side of his lapels like he's posing for someone to take his photo. Finally, he says, "As a registered voter, you should be ashamed of yourself, Mr. Cole."

Oh great. He's a politician. No, not just any politician. I've seen his face on television for years now.

Holy shit!

This dude is the fucking governor of North Carolina!

He strolls into the room until he's standing right in front of me, then holds out his hand. "Lawrence Washington."

Southern-bred hospitality takes over as I blink at him and I shake his hand.

Once my brain catches up, I realize that this, him showing up here, is really bad.

"Should I be honored that the governor is checking in on me? I doubt you're here to ask me to vote for you in November. Incarcerated felons can't exactly make it out to the polls."

"Well, if all goes as planned, you won't be incarcerated in November," he tells me. "Have a seat, Mr. Cole." Then, over his shoulder, he says, "Can I get a chair in here and maybe a meal and beverage for our guest?"

Guest? What, like we're having a tea party or some shit? I'm a fucking prisoner.

"What is this about?" I ask him, my patience wearing thin. Although, if he comes through on this food and beverage request, he could possibly be my new best friend.

"Let's get something in your stomach before we get down to business," he says. "Negotiations are always more likely to succeed after a decent meal."

"Negotiations?" I repeat, but the politician remains tight lipped as he stands with his hands clasped behind his back and waits for his requests to be met.

A suit carries in a food tray, and the smell of a big, juicy cheeseburger hits me before I see it. I snatch it up and sink my teeth into it a second later.

"Mmm. God, that's good," I moan as I chew, savoring the flavor even though it's room temperature at best.

"I'm not god, but I have my sights set on the presidency," the governor says while I eat like a starving animal. I suppose it would be polite to slow down and listen, but I really don't give two shits what he thinks. I'm too hungry to care. And thirsty. Fuck, I'm thirsty. That's when I spot the enormous white fast food lidded cup with a straw. I don't care if it's pink lemonade in that bitch, I reach for it and guzzle it down.

"Sweet tea. Nice," I say when I pause long enough to taste it. The beverage is so cool and refreshing that I almost forget I've been locked in a prison cell. *Almost.*

"Have a seat, and let's talk while you eat," Washington says, his hand gesturing to the uncomfortable cot just as one of the other guys brings in a gray metal folding chair and opens it for him.

By the time he lowers his ass to sit down, I've finished my burger, half my tea, and have grabbed the fries from the tray, eating them one at a time as I grip them with my teeth since I refuse to give up the cup.

"That'll be all for now," the governor tells the men, and they all leave us, shutting the door behind them. The clanking slam of it reminds me that just because he fed me doesn't mean I get to leave anytime soon. Although, he did say something about not being incarcerated in November if I cooperate...

No, fuck that. It can't be that easy unless he wants me to cough up some criminal details to lock up my brothers in the Savage Kings. That won't ever happen.

"So, let's hear your spiel," I tell him, followed by a long, disgusting burp orchestrated just to annoy him. "I appreciate the grub, but I can save you some time if you want. My answer will be no to whatever you ask."

"Don't you want to hear it first?"

Picking up another fry with my teeth, I chew it up and then finally sit down on the cot like he wanted. Once I swallow, I say, "I just want to know what charges you've got me locked up for."

"Serious ones I'm afraid," he replies, resting his palms on his thighs. "Federal, of course. You're a smart man with a few years of college under your belt. I'm sure you've heard of the Racketeer Influenced and Corrupted Organizations Act, also known as the acronym RICO."

"What about it?" I ask, refusing to give him any details.

"You and every single one of your MC buddies are in hot water for a multitude of organized crimes."

"Like what? Right now it just sounds like you're full of shit and are trying to use me as part of your fishing expedition."

"Oh, there's no need for me to try and fish for information. I have plenty of specifics, if that's what you want from me," he says as he pulls his cell phone from inside his suit jacket. "Conspiracy, to start with."

"Conspiracy?" I repeat. "I've got a squeaky-clean record. Our attorney can get most of us off with a slap on the wrist for any of your little marijuana charges."

"Marijuana, right," the governor says. "No one gives a shit about you all growing and distributing weed."

"Oh really? Because that whole DEA arrest earlier where I was thrown in here makes me think someone gives a shit."

"I had to bring you in, and those federal agents were willing to help me," Washington says with a shrug. Leaning forward, he lowers his voice and says, "The thing is, the feds don't know about the Savage Kings MC's conspiracy to commit the murders of twenty Russian nationals yet."

Oh shit.

"I don't know what the hell you're talking about," I bluff.

"Well," he says with a sigh while punching keys on his phone. "Maybe this little video taken outside the Escapades strip club in Greensboro will refresh your memory."

I'm still in shock from hearing him cough up those very specific details about our slaughter a few weeks ago when he flips his phone around to show me the screen. Then, I watch a silent video of myself and all the other Kings minus Reece and Cooper, who stayed here in town while Cynthia was recovering, marching into the club.

"Let me give you the spoilers since it's a long video," the governor says. "About an hour or so after you all go inside, the Russian mob boss Boris Kozlov and nineteen of his men walk in, but only the Savage Kings and Anthony Russo, or Ivan Rivers, as you probably know him, come out."

"Guess the Russians really liked the strippers and stayed overnight," I lie.

"Oh no, they didn't stay overnight," Washington replies. He turns the phone's screen around; and then when he shows it to me again, it's a video of several men carrying black garbage bags from the back of the building and throwing them into the back of a food truck. The video is mostly green tinted with night vision or some shit, but it's still clear.

How? How the fuck did he get a video of all of this? Eddie and Cedric checked for cameras on nearby buildings, and Ivan assured us that there were none in the alley. It doesn't make sense!

"I bet you're wondering how we obtained such an interesting video," the governor says, reading my mind as he locks the phone's screen and puts it away in his suit jacket. "Drones."

"Drones?" I repeat.

"Technology is simply amazing, isn't it?" he asks. "Those little cameras can fly right above, say, a convoy of Harleys, without detection."

"All you have is a video of dudes going to a strip club. The only thing you could do with that as 'evidence' is piss off a couple of wives," I mutter.

"But you see, we also *followed* the food truck to the landfill, which would be strange enough on its own, and were able to find a few of those black garbage bags."

Son of a motherfucker!

Whispering, he asks, "You know what we found in those trash bags? The severed body parts of a bunch of dead Russian men."

The burger, fries and tea I scarfed down start to turn heavy in my stomach. In fact, I'm not sure I can keep them down much longer.

"Great! Now it looks like you're ready to hear my proposition," Governor Washington says as he leans back in his chair. "I'm willing to make the evidence I just showed you disappear before the feds get their hands on it *and* call in a few favors to get them to drop the marijuana trafficking charges against you and your MC buddies if you agree to do one little thing for me," he says. "Do you really want to spend the rest of your life behind bars? Do you want your 'brothers' to all spend their lives in prison? That would be a shame since some of them have small children and babies on the way..."

Jesus Christ.

Not only would the guys be miserable if they got arrested and convicted on these murders, their women would be devastated. And their kids – War's son, Torin's boy and girl, Miles' kid on the way – they'll be raised fatherless, which would destroy their families. If there's anything I can do to prevent that, I have to, right? Not just to save my own ass, but everyone I know and care about.

"You see, Mr. Cole, I don't actually *want* to throw you and your MC guys in prison for the rest of your lives. You took out the trash, literally, stopping one of the main sources of heroin from coming into my state, and saving tax payers tons of money since law enforcement and the court system didn't have to get involved. But I'm not opposed to making the call to the US Attorney and turning over my evidence either. Either way is a win for me," he says with a shrug of his shoulders.

"What the fuck do you want?" I ask since we both know he's got me by the balls.

"It's simple really. I just need someone like you to watch out for my daughter."

"I'm not a babysitter," I tell him.

"Isobel is not a baby. She's twenty-eight."

Brows drawn together because I'm completely lost, I ask, "Then why do you need me to watch out for a grown ass woman?"

"Because she shouldn't be on her own in the world without protection," he says.

"Then hire a bodyguard."

"You think I haven't tried?" he huffs. "She refuses to let me keep a man on her. And to top it all off, she keeps losing the guards I covertly assign to her, constantly staying on the move. I just need you to try and slow her down."

"I don't understand," I confess.

"You'll meet her in a bar, buy her a drink, and go from there," he says with a wave of his hand.

When he stays silent after that statement, a bark of laughter escapes me. "Are you asking me to fuck your daughter? God, you're certifiably insane! How the hell did you ever get elected?"

"Because I do what needs to be done to keep the people in *my* state safe," he growls, face reddening as he loses his temper for the first time in our conversation. "I won't do any less for Isobel!"

"You're serious," I remark in disbelief. "All I have to do to get my ass and my brothers out of *life* sentences is screw your little girl? That's got to be the strangest request ever made by a fucking father," I tell him with a disgusted shake of my head.

"I need Isobel to settle down, to put down roots before time runs out."

"Time? What time is running out?" I ask before it hits me. "*Ohhh!* You mean you need your daughter to be grounded where you can keep an eye on her, so she won't fuck up your re-election campaign. That's fucking low, man."

"My daughter has been going through a rough patch, that's all," he says defensively. "I know what's best for her, and I can take care of her if she'll just stop living her life like it's one big party."

"And I'm somehow supposed to be the man to make her stop partying and help you and your public image?"

"Isobel has always preferred men of your...caliber."

"You mean she's a good girl who loves bad boys, huh?" I ask with a grin.

"You're not *all* bad though, are you, Saxon? How exactly did you become a member of the Savage Kings?" he questions me.

"I prospected for a year just like everyone else."

"No, I think it was a little something more than that." He stares me down, waiting for me to break. He can wait forever because I've never told anyone what I did, and I never will.

When I refuse to respond, Washington says, "Have you forgotten? It has been twelve years or so, but you told DEA Agent Green that the Emerald Isle Savage Kings MC members were responsible for your girlfriend's death, and that *you* were going to prove it."

Swallowing around the boulder that's suddenly lodged in my throat at the mention of April, I tell him, "I was wrong." *How the hell does he know all of this shit?*

"Maybe so, but do the Savage Kings know you started out in their organization as a confidential informant for the feds? I wonder what they would say when they find out..."

"Yeah, well, I wonder what your voters would fucking say about you trying to blackmail me!"

"Nice try, Mr. Cole, but you would have to air out all your dirty laundry to blow the whistle on me. Are you willing to risk losing everything, including your life, to try and take me down? Your word over mine?"

"I'm probably dead either way, right? The Kings will kill me if you tell them or if they find out I agreed to work for you."

"Then they never have to know. You have my word," he says, holding out his palm for me to shake like we've made an agreement.

I'm fucked upside down and sideways and the asshole knows it. Goddamn him to hell.

Blowing out a heavy exhale, I refuse to shake his hand, but I do ask, "What does she look like?"

"My daughter? Oh, Isobel is beautiful, just like her mother was," he responds before he retrieves his phone again and then shows me her photo.

She's so petite she looks much younger than twenty-eight. Maybe that's just because in the picture she's crouching down, surrounded by a bunch of Little Orphan Annie kids in tattered clothes and covered in dirt like they're homeless or something. Despite their circumstances, they're all hugging her tightly like she's some sort of heaven-sent angel. And no wonder.

The governor lied about his daughter.

She's not beautiful.

She's so fucking gorgeous that she practically emits an ethereal glow.

"Isobel is a pediatric nurse. That picture was taken last year when she was vaccinating kids for polo in Mozambique."

Wow, she's the picture-perfect daughter for a politician, saving under-privileged kids and shit.

"I'm pretty sure that I'm not this woman's type," I tell the governor.

"She's not currently working in the nursing field or saving children."

"Then what is she doing?

"Drinking in bars and going home with a man in a different city every night."

"Wow. How did she go from a baby nurse to a slut overnight?" I ask, and his fist socks me right in the mouth a half a second later. Not that I didn't have it coming, but still, I'm surprised that the cool, calm politician snapped.

"You will treat my daughter with respect, or I'll kill you myself!" he threatens me as I run my tongue over my teeth to make sure they're all there. Thankfully, none are missing, but I'm pretty sure there's a cut on my lip.

"Respect her or fuck her? Pretty hard to do both," I respond.

"Your job is to figure it out from now until the election in November. I want her to return to nursing and to let me back into her life. Convince her of both of those things if you want to keep your life and your brothers to retain their freedom," he says before he straightens his suit jacket and starts towards the door. After he pounds his fist on it wordlessly three times, he turns back to me and says, "Oh, and one more thing. Other than the two of us, there's only one other person who will know what you're doing with Isobel. I insist we keep it that way."

"Oh yeah? Who else knows?" I ask while I reach up to wipe a drop of blood from my lips with my fingertips as I let his demands sink in.

"Ian Long."

My entire body freezes.

Fuck. Having a Savage King in the know is not good.

"Ian turned you down, didn't he? Is that why he's not out of prison yet? He was supposed to be released months ago, but then there was some sort of 'altercation'!"

"I didn't have enough dirt on him," Washington responds. "All I could offer Long was an early release and to keep one of his secrets from the MC. He refused by spitting on me," he says with his lip curled in disgust. "One of the guards saw it, so the warden threw him in solitary and put it down as an assault, which cost him his good behavior time."

Shit. Has Ian told anyone in the MC yet? I need to see him ASAP to find out.

"If I do this, I want you to let Ian out," I say to the governor. "He deserves it, and it would give me a bargaining chip to make sure he doesn't tell any of our brothers."

"Here's another bargaining chip free of charge," he replies. "According to one of the prison guards, Ian's been paying him off for unauthorized, private conjugal visits on the regular. It wasn't enough blackmail for him to give in to my request, but it's not something he probably wants his MC brothers to know."

"So what? Why would the MC give a shit if he's getting some ass in prison?" I ask with my brow furrowed. The poor guy has been locked up for almost five years. The dude deserves to get his dick wet every once in a while.

"Well," the governor drawls. "For one, the conjugals have all been with a man. And secondly, he also happens to be a member of the Savage Kings."

My jaw drops in surprise because of what he's implying. And without any further information I'm pretty sure I know exactly *which* King has been visiting Ian during that private time.

"He didn't visibly flinch when I threatened to out him, but I could tell he wasn't looking forward to that information reaching his 'friends'. That information should prove useful to deter Mr. Long from discussing our arrangement with the other members, don't you think?"

"Ah, yeah. I guess so," I say even though I would never out Ian and Gabe to the Kings, no matter what fucking happens. Doesn't mean I'm above using the threat for leverage.

"If you succeed in this endeavor, then I'll process Mr. Long's paperwork," Washington agrees.

"And how will you know if I succeed?" I ask.

"My daughter won't step foot out of North Carolina again before the election. Not unless she's treating kids in impoverished nations with a photographer capturing every second. You'll also need to persuade her to get her job back and try to repair our relationship. If you fail to make those things happen, I'll put you and the rest of your gang in cells right next to your friend, Ian."

Fuck me. I'm actually going to do this shit for him. But what other choice do I have? Besides, manipulating a woman I've never met and don't give two shits about sounds easy compared to life in prison for everyone I care about.

"How do I find her?" I ask our state's dickhead leader just as the cell door swings open.

"I have the number to the burner phone they seized from your boat yesterday. I'll send you the address of the next bar she's sighted at. Isobel was recently spotted in Georgia, so I'm predicting she'll be in South Carolina this week. That will give you the perfect chance to swoop in and stop her from leaving again." Then, to the men in suits, he says, "We struck a deal, so he's free to go. I've already cleared it with Agent Green. You can call him if you need to."

Great, it looks like I'm a free man again.

Or at least as free as I get to be for the next few months while I'm stuck under the governor's fucking thumb.

CHAPTER THREE

Sax

"Hey, man. How you been?" I ask when the guards bring Ian into the visitation room and we clasp hands and slap each other on the back. The dude was thick before prison, but now he's massive. Guess there's not much to do other than workout. And apparently fuck around with Gabe...

"I'm as good as I can get in here," Ian replies before taking a seat in one of the chairs at the empty table next to us. "After a stint in solitary, being back in the cellblock is almost as good as being home."

"I heard about the, ah, 'altercation' with a certain politician," I tell him. "That's actually why I'm here."

"Jesus fuck," Ian groans as he slouches in his seat. "What do they have on you?"

"Evidence," I reply, leaving out the fact that he's blackmailing me about my past. "Not just evidence to implicate me, and all but two of the Kings. It's serious, man."

"So you caved, huh?" he asks.

"What choice did I fucking have? We're all looking at life without parole."

"Life?" he repeats with his eyebrow raised. "No shit? All of the Kings?"

"Life for everyone, well, except for Reece and Cooper," I say again. "But they could take them down with RICO too."

"Even Gabriel could, you know, get life?" he asks in concern. The two are obviously closer than everyone thought.

"Ah, yeah. He was there that night."

"Fuck. Then I guess you have to do what you have to do; right, bro?"

"Yeah, I do," I agree. "And I was hoping we could, ah, just keep this between us. Did you tell anyone about the governor's visit yet?"

"Nope," he mutters. "Only Gabe visits on the regular, and he couldn't come while I was in the hole."

I try not to let my reaction show that I'm well aware of *exactly* what takes place on those visits with Gabe that involves coming and holes. I think I can trust Ian without throwing that sort of personal shit in his face as blackmail. If or when him and Gabe are ready to tell us what's going on, I'm sure they will. Until then, I'll keep their secret.

"Okay, good," I say in relief. "I'm gonna do what the asshole wants, and then we'll all be free and clear, even you."

"I don't want jack shit from that prick," Ian huffs.

"Aren't you ready to get the hell out of here? It's been too long, man."

"And what exactly will I come home to? I barely have a penny to my name after spending everything I had on a worthless attorney."

"You know you can stay at the clubhouse however long you need."

"Where? In someone's bathtub? All the rooms are taken."

"No, most are empty now," I inform him. "All the guys are shacking up with their old ladies. Hasn't Gabe told you?"

Chuckling as his eyes dart away, he says, "You know how our boy is. I come in the room and the fucking waterworks turn on, so I end up talking about the shiv of the week and shit."

Right. Guess they don't have much time for talking when they're doing other things together.

"Gabe's a sensitive guy who looked up to you when you sponsored him. He hates seeing you in here," I respond. "We all do."

"Yeah, well, it's on me. I fucked up getting caught with heat on me, now I have to do the time."

"You're getting out of here, and soon," I assure him. I won't let him and the other guys down; because if I fail, not only will Ian stay behind bars, we'll all be joining him.

"Don't worry about me. I can take care of myself."

"Yeah, I know," I reply. "But it would be good to have you back at the table again."

Before he can respond, my phone buzzes in my pocket. Pulling it out, I read the new text message.

"Shit. Speak of the devil..." I start.

"You gotta split?" Ian asks.

"I better get on the road and get down to Myrtle Beach to take care of business."

"Do what you need to do, but watch your ass," he says. "You can't trust this prick. One favor will lead to another; and before you know it, he'll own your ass."

"That's never gonna happen," I assure him, even though I honestly have no idea how to ensure the governor won't keep holding this shit over my head in the future and asking for more favors if I succeed.

THE BIKER BAR on the strip is the last place I expected to find the governor's daughter. Tonight, it's so packed that I have to park my bike in the Huddle House parking lot and walk over. I can hear the hoots and hollers of drunken men over the music from across the street. One good thing I notice when I step inside the packed room is that at least I don't have to worry about standing out. The majority of the patrons are also wearing denim or leather cuts with MC patches. Hell, some of the guys playing pool are even local Savage Kings. I steer clear of them, though, and head to the bar to start searching for the woman in the picture the governor sent me along with the address. A girl on stage angrily belts out Joan Jett and the Black-hearts "I Hate Myself for Loving You" much to the rowdy crowd's delight.

"What can I get you?" the giant, bald bartender comes over and asks.

"Bottle of Miller Lite," I answer. Then, before he turns away, I pull out my phone and ask, "Have you seen this woman in here tonight?" His dark eyes narrow to look closer at the photo on the screen. His head tilts to the side and then he grins. "Why, yes, I have."

"Is she still here?"

"Uh-huh."

"So where can I find her?" I ask, getting annoyed with his runaround.

"On stage," he replies. "Although she looks a little different with the blue hair. An improvement, if you ask me."

"On stage?" I repeat as I swivel around on my bar stool to face the front of the room, the center of every man's attention. And now I see why.

Fuck me. The angry little singer is sexy as hell. She's a petite, five foot nothing even in her four-inch black heels with long, wavy, turquoise hair that falls nearly to her narrow waist. In fact, her hair probably covers more skin than the black leather zipper dress she's wearing. Her eyes are heavy with smoky makeup, and her lips are thick and sensual as she belts out the well-known rock 'n roll lyrics.

That's the governor's daughter?

If her hair was brown and you remove all the makeup, then yeah,

I think I can see the resemblance of the young woman in the photo to the singer.

No longer the sweet girl saving children, now she could easily pass for a pin-up girl from Easy Riders' magazine. No fucking wonder Washington wants someone to tame her. If the press got their hands on a pic of her like this, singing on stage, he'd probably have a stroke.

As a man, I can definitely appreciate her sexy show; but for some unknown reason, there's a small part of me that would love to throw a long trench coat over her body to cover up her cleavage and mouth-watering thigh gap from the lecherous eyes of all the men currently gawking at her.

"Here you go," the bartender says from behind me. "That'll be three bucks, man."

It takes me several long moments to pull my eyes from the singer's sensual dance moves to finally fish the money from my wallet to pay up.

Grabbing my beer, I swivel back around to face the stage. The crowd noise dies down when the rock goddess speaks to them with her fingers wrapped erotically around the mic. Grinning, she says, "We're gonna slow things down for you wild boys. This next song is dedicated to the sad, hungover women who'll wake up beside your ugly asses tomorrow."

Deep rumbling laughter fills the air as one of the guys on stage brings over a stool and places it in front of the microphone stand. The siren climbs up on it daintily and crosses her legs; then someone hands her an acoustic guitar that she begins to strum.

She sings the first few words so softly into the mic that I don't have a fucking clue what the song is. All I know is that the hairs on my arms are standing straight up because she has the most beautiful voice I've ever heard. Her notes rise gradually as the drums come in, and then she closes her eyes and croons the familiar chorus of "Angel of the Morning."

When those smoky eyes of hers eventually reopen, I swear they land right on me even though I'm at least twenty-feet from the stage in a crowded sea of people. I'm certain I must be mistaken, that she's just looking in my general direction. But her piercing gaze locks with mine until the very last note, paralyzing me and making my heart skip a few beats.

There haven't been many moments in my life that have stayed with me in excruciating detail – the first time I rode a bike *and* a Harley without dropping it, when I walked across the stage to accept my high school diploma, the night I was given my Savage Kings' patch, and the phone call I had with April's parents when they told me she was gone. But without a doubt, tonight there will be another unforgettable memory seared into my brain – the first time I saw and heard an angel sing.

CHAPTER FOUR

Isobel

"Thank you so much for having me tonight! Rock on, Myrtle Beach!" I tell the crowd after my set; then walk off stage ready to grab a cold drink and cool off. Maybe I'll even get to talk to the blond biker sitting at the bar, the one I could feel staring at me through the entire last song. Plenty of men look at me with desire in their eyes while I'm on stage, but this guy was...different. It felt like he could actually *see* me, who I am underneath the costume and makeup. I wasn't just a random singer to him. The stricken look on his face said I was someone he recognized even though we've never met before. I would've definitely remembered him if we had.

"You were fucking amazing, Izzie," Tim, the drummer, says when he follows me off stage, his blue t-shirt drenched in sweat.

"I appreciate you guys letting me sing with you. It was fun," I tell him while crouching down to put my guitar back into the case. Now

I'm only three states away from my goal of singing on stage in all fifty.

"Just fun?" he says when I stand back up and face him. "Why the hell don't you do this for a living? I bet record labels would be lining up to sign you if they heard you sing."

"Eh, I'm not interested in any deals or tours," I assure him. "There's too much I want to see and do in the world. I don't want *anyone* holding me back, especially not some label telling me how to live every second of my life."

"Yeah, but the money would be awesome," he replies with a grin as he rubs his finger and thumb together.

"They may pay out millions, but then they own you. No one is *ever* going to own me again."

"I hear ya," he says with his palms up in the air. "If I didn't have to get back out there, I would offer to buy you a drink."

"Next time I'm in town maybe," I say. "See ya, Tim."

"Bye, Izzie," he says with a smile before heading back on stage, leaving me alone in the hallway.

That's the thing about traveling around so much, I spend a lot of time alone. Sure, I've met some great people, but they're only temporary. We're ships passing in the night or whatever, sometimes literally. After practically being a nun for the first twenty-some years of my life that I spent with my nose buried in books, I have a lot of catching up to do in the bedroom. And it's nice to be close to another human being for a few hours, even though I know I'll be leaving them behind as soon as the sun comes up.

Picking up my guitar case and throwing on my crossbody hobo purse, I head out the back entrance of the bar and into the darkness, reveling in the coastal breeze as it whips strands of my hair around into my face. In fact, I'm so distracted by the cool night air that I don't notice I'm *not* alone until a strong hand clamps down on my bare shoulder.

"Back off!" I yell as I whirl around on the stranger, slamming the end of my guitar case into their knees.

"Shit," the short man in khakis and a dark polo shirt curses. When he glances up, I get a good look at his face and let out a breath of relief since I recognize him.

"What are you doing here, Stu?" I ask my father's main henchman.

"Sorry to startle you, Miss Washington, but I need you to come with me," he says when he places his hand on my forearm that's still holding the case. "I'm afraid your father insists."

A huff of laughter is my first response to his statement. "My father can *insist* all he wants, but I'm not going anywhere with you," I tell him. "Now get your hand off of me," I order through gritted teeth as I try to break free from his grip. He only squeezes my arm tighter.

"Yo, asshole, does she need to draw you a picture?" a deep voice asks from behind us. I squint at the figure approaching but can't make out many of his features. The street lamps behind him are casting his face into shadow as he strolls over to us. He's tall, broad-shouldered and wearing leather, which usually means trouble. The next thing I know, he's wielding a big ass knife and pressing it across Stu's throat as he gets in his face. "Take your fucking hand off her before I slice your head clear off your body."

Whoa! That's one harsh threat from the stranger, but it works. Stu releases my arm and even takes a step backward, most likely to get the knife blade further away from his jugular.

"Go home, Stu. Be sure to remind my father that I'm not a dog and I don't appreciate being treated like one," I say to try and diffuse the situation before my dark knight decides to draw blood.

"H-his birthday dinner is tomorrow night at seven," Stu informs me. "He would love for you to come."

"I'm sure he would," I mutter. "Take care, Stu." Giving up, probably because he realizes it's a lost cause, my father's errand runner finally turns around and leaves, heading to the street to try and cross the busy highway.

"Um, so thanks, but he wasn't going to hurt me or anything," I tell the stranger, watching as he closes and puts his potential murder weapon back into the knife holster on his belt. His arms are bare, making the glow of the streetlight dance along his thick, chiseled biceps as the muscles flex with his movements.

"No problem," he responds. "But I wasn't going to actually hurt him. Well, unless he kept on insisting."

When I lift my eyes to his face, he's grinning down at me in such a playful, friendly way that I think I imagined his violent display just moments earlier. It's pretty dark out here, but I would almost swear he's the same blond man I saw from the stage. That's highly unlikely, though.

"Right, of course not. You were just posturing," I say sarcastically. "I bet that knife of yours wasn't even real."

"Totally a fake. I've just been carrying it around, hoping for the chance to come to a beautiful woman's rescue."

"Oh, so that was like your pickup line?" I ask, unable to prevent my lips from forming into a smile.

"Exactly," he says, slipping his hands into his pockets to try and appear more casual and less threatening. Damn, if it doesn't work too. Now he just looks like a good ole southern boy with a handsome, easygoing face and a rock-hard body.

"Well, it worked much better than just coming up and asking if you can buy me a drink."

"If you think about it, it's a pretty genius plan. Now I bet you want to buy *me* a drink as a thank you for running off that grabby jackass."

He's obviously flirting with me; and while the good girl in me knows deep down he's a dangerous guy I shouldn't waste another minute on, the inner bad girl I've been embracing recently wants to go back into the bar and see where things go with him. Even if it doesn't work out, I can always search for the blond biker I locked eyes with from the stage.

"Okay," I agree. "Let me put my guitar case in my car and then I'll buy you a drink."

Reaching down, he takes the case from my hand and whispers, "Should I be worried about you slipping a roofie in my beer so you can take advantage of me?"

"How else am I supposed to seduce a man like you?" I joke.

Sighing heavily, he says, "Guess I'll have to take my chances. Besides, you're too pretty to have to drug men. You had every guy in the bar eating out of your hand."

"You must be the bravest of them all," I tell him with a shake of my head as I dig around in my purse to find my car keys.

"I'm Sax, by the way, in case you like to keep records of your victims."

"Sax?" I repeat as I start for my white Lexus. "Like sex but with an 'A'?"

"Yeah, short for Saxon."

"Okay, that's unique," I say, popping the trunk for him to place my guitar case inside. "I'm Izzie."

"Is Izzie short for Isabella or Isobel?"

"Isobel," I reply.

"It's nice to meet you, Isobel," Sax says, then slams the trunk down. "Now, how about you go buy me that drink and then tell me what the hell that scene with the old guy was all about?"

"You sure you want to hear about my family drama?" I ask as we start back around to the front of the bar.

"Why wouldn't I?" he questions me.

"You just look like the type who only wants to talk about motor-cycles and whatever else gets women out of their panties."

His chuckle is rumbly and hot, quaking all the way through my lower belly.

"We can postpone the motorcycle and panty-dropping conversa-tions until later," Sax replies, holding open the door for me to go inside the noisy bar first. "What was that dude saying about your dad when he was trying to drag you away?"

"That's par for the course when it comes to my father, wanting me to go where he wants, when he wants it," I explain, eager to see his face in full light when he joins me in the bar. And holy shit! It is him! My dark knight is the blond biker. I felt a pull to him on stage; and after talking to him, that connection is definitely growing stronger.

Oh crap.

What were we talking about? My mind completely blanks as I stare at Sax. Up close, I can see the dark blond scruff along his square jaw that ups his hotness factor even higher. His eyes are light, but I can't tell if they're blue or green. He's even more attractive face to face, that's for sure.

Realizing I've been gawking at him for too long, I shake my head and finally remember where I left off on our conversation. He was asking about what Stu wanted. And for whatever reason, I find myself opening up to him like he's a longtime friend and not a knife-toting stranger. "For over twenty years, I let my father control every aspect of my life. All he cares about is orchestrating perfect appearances. So now, I only do what *I* want to do, which drives him crazy."

"And what is it that you want to do?" Sax asks when we find two empty stools at the bar and climb up on them next to each other.

"Right now, tonight? No clue." Reaching down into my purse that's still hanging across the front of my body, I pull out my tiny spiral notebook that's covered with cherry blossoms and has an equally tiny pink pen attached to the spine. Handing it to Sax, I say, "Here. You tell me. Spontaneity is my new best friend."

"What's this?" he asks as he thumbs through the pages.

"My bucket list."

"Aren't you a little young to have one of these?" he questions, holding up the notebook with one blond eyebrow arched. And for the first time, I'm able to finally see the color of his eyes. They're a beautiful, sparkling sky blue, reminding me of the ocean in the morning when the sun shines down, making the surface of the water glisten. It even takes me several seconds to remember his question yet again. Oh, right, why does someone my age have a bucket list. I'm not usually so absentminded but gazing at Sax for too long could probably make me forget my name.

Instead of giving him the depressing truth behind my bucket list, I tell him, "It's never too early to start living like you might die tomorrow. Why have a shitload of regrets on your deathbed when you could have done everything you dreamed of before you die?"

"Very true," he agrees with a crooked grin while staring at my face. Eventually, he clears his throat and drops his gaze back to the notebook.

"Tonight you can help me cross something off," I say as he reads over the entries. "I mean, if you want to..."

"Fuck yes," Sax agrees. "I am all for helping you..." He flips a few pages before picking. "*Participate in an orgy.*"

"Try again buddy," I tell him with a roll of my eyes.

Chuckling aloud, he keeps reading as he asks, "So tonight, when you were on stage, was that something you were crossing off your list, or is it what you do for a living?"

"You saw that, huh?" I ask, even though I caught him staring.

"Don't act like you weren't thinking about waking up in my bed while you were singing that last song," he says when he looks back up at me with a knowing look in his eyes, calling my bluff. "Every man in here was picturing you in their bed. In fact, I may have to break out that fake knife of mine again to ward off a few admirers who are still gawking at you."

"No way," I tell him. "Watch this." I swivel around, putting my back to Sax and smiling at the burly, bearded man next to me when he glances over.

"Hello darlin'. You have got an incredible set of lungs. How about you let me buy you a drink?" he asks. "Bartender!"

"Absolutely!" I agree. When the bartender turns his attention to us, I tell him, "I'll have a vodka tonic, and my boyfriend would like..." Turning to Sax, I ask, "Hey, babe. What do you want to drink?"

Chuckling while trying to hide it as a cough, he says, "Miller Lite would be great."

"A vodka tonic and a Miller Lite," I inform the bartender. "Thank you so much for treating us," I say to the burly biker, placing a hand on his shoulder.

With a grunt, he tosses down a twenty-dollar bill and then stomps off toward the pool table.

"That was cruel," Sax says through his laughter. "But I have to say, it is the first time a bear has bought me a drink. I'm kind of flattered."

"Just one of the perks of being my fake boyfriend," I reply with a grin.

"Fake boyfriend, huh?" he says with his sexy, crooked smile. "Wouldn't you love to see the look on your father's face if you brought home a man like me?"

"Oh my god," I mutter as I imagine it. "You have to meet my father!" I tell him. "He would flip out if I brought home someone like you tomorrow night."

Sax's smile turns upside down in the blink of an eye at the same time my notebook falls from his hands onto the bar, making me nearly fall off my chair from cackling. "Jeez! You should see your face! Hilarious!"

"You *were* joking, right?" he asks as the bartender places our drinks in front of us.

"No, I was totally serious," I say while picking up my tumbler and taking a sip from the straw.

"You want me to meet your father? After we just met, like, ten minutes ago?" he says in a rush, then guzzles half of his beer.

"Yes, I do. I've never been more certain of anything in my life. Lately, I live to piss off my father in as many creative ways as I can. I wasn't planning to go to his birthday dinner or whatever tomorrow, but now...I'm sort of looking forward to it."

"Oh yeah? Why's that?" Sax asks.

"Because he has done nothing but manipulate me from the day I was born," I admit. "My life wasn't ever my own. But he's such an expert at manipulation that I didn't even realize what he was doing until I finally caught him in one enormous lie!"

"Damn. It sounds like you hate his guts."

"I do," I agree.

"Then why would you want to see him on his birthday?" he questions.

"Because...I don't know," I say, sipping my drink and biding my time while I try to figure out how to explain it to a stranger. "Because he's the only family I have left. So, while I can't stand to see his face or hear his annoying nagging about my life choices, I would love to bring you along just to piss him off."

Sax is silent for so long, I glance back over to make sure he's still sitting next to me.

"Okay, I'll go with you to see your dad," he says.

"You will? You can be on your worst behavior. In fact, nothing would make me happier than seeing the look on his face when he meets you."

"Sounds...fun," he replies, the biggest lie I've ever heard.

"If you're serious about doing this for me, maybe I'll do something nice for you," I tell him, leaning over to bump his shoulder with mine.

"Oh really? Like what?" he asks.

Tapping a fingernail on the top of my bucket list notebook, I say, "Like let you pick *anything* on my bucket list to cross off, even the orgy."

"Deal," Sax quickly agrees. "You're a kickass negotiator, by the way."

"Ugh," I groan. "I get that from my father, unfortunately."

Before I can dwell on that, he asks, "So, what about tonight? Have you decided what you want to do yet?"

"You tell me. I'm down for a little PG-13 fun."

"Gotta keep it PG-13 tonight, huh?" he asks as his eyes lower to the zipper on the front of my leather dress. I just know a million dirty thoughts are likely running through his filthy mind. He may very well get lucky tonight, but I don't plan to make it *too* easy for him.

"Well, yeah. I just met you in a bar. What kind of girl do you take me for?" I ask, feigning indignation.

"The beautiful, sexy, mysterious kind who somehow talked me into meeting her father on our first date," Sax answers with a devious grin.

"And what kind of guy are you?"

Glancing around the bar before his eyes lock with mine, he says, "The outlaw biker kind with so many skeletons hiding in my closet you would run in the opposite direction of me if you were smart."

Shaking my head, I tell him, "I tried being the smart, good girl, but it didn't really work out. Wasn't much fun either." Leaning forward, I plant one of my palms on his upper thigh. Then, digging my nails into the denim, I whisper against his ear, "Now I prefer to be a little bad."

Sax

I TOLD myself I wasn't going to fuck Isobel. It's not right to enjoy myself while in the process of fucking her over for her father to save the guys.

But that was before I met her and had her lips brush over my ear, sending a jolt of lust right down to my cock.

Now, about the only thing I *can* think about is getting her naked and sinking inside of her.

Screw it. I'm already going to hell. What does one more blemish on my record really matter in the big scheme of things?

Sleeping with Isobel isn't worse than participating in a mass murder with the other Kings just a few weeks ago.

And it's not even close to being as shitty as betraying my brothers from day one.

Still, even after twelve years I'm not sure if I really think of the Savage Kings as *my* brothers. I'm a fraud who somehow ended up not only getting patched in, but also got elected as an officer by them. As the mother charter's secretary, I'm in charge of notifying members of shitstorms, planning how to take cover during said storms, and making sure the other charters stay in one piece. That's a helluva lot of responsibility for a man who once had a goal to send every last member wearing the bearded skull king to prison.

At the time, I was young, stupid and angry. I was also hurting and wanted someone to pay for ending April's life before it had really started.

"You okay?" Isobel asks, her beautiful face frowning at me when my eyes refocus on her.

"Yeah," I reply and have to clear my throat to get any other words out of it. "I was just thinking of a few PG-13 activities we could get into tonight."

"And? What's the verdict?" she asks, biting on her lip as she waits for my decision.

"Have you ever ridden a Harley?"

"No, I have not, but it is on my list," she tells me, flipping to the item in her little book.

"Good. What do you say we check that one off, and I take you out on my boat?"

"You have a boat?" she asks with both of her eyebrows raised in surprise. "I didn't have you pegged as a sailor."

"Good, because I don't sail," I respond. "And on my boat, I prefer to be called 'Captain'."

"Right," Isobel drawls with a roll of her iridescent hazel eyes when she tosses her bucket list back into her purse. "I just need to do one little thing before we take off on your Harley and hit the seas on your boat."

"What's that?" I ask.

Holding out her hand, palm up, she says, "Could I please see your driver's license?"

"What? Why?" I ask, going on the defensive even though there's nothing on my ID that will give away my big fat lie to her.

"If I'm going to be alone with a man I just met in a bar, I have to have some sort of collateral on him," she explains. "The easiest way to do that is to snap a photo of your license and send it to my friend, Daniel. We've known each other since high school, and his father is the Chief of Police in Cary. Then, if he doesn't hear from me again after twelve hours, an APB goes out."

"Oh, damn. Aren't you resourceful and shit?"

"Single women have to be careful nowadays," she responds with a shrug of her shoulders while I dig my leather wallet out of my back pocket. I pull out my ID from inside without removing the wallet from the chain attached to my belt loop. "There you go," I tell Isobel when I slap the plastic down on the bar in front of her.

"Thanks," she says before her phone is over top of it taking a picture. Her fingers fly over the keys and then I hear the whooshing sound of a text being sent. "There. Now Daniel will know who to look for if I go missing or turn up dead!"

"Do I look like a serial killer?" I ask her.

"You're charming and handsome, so yes, you would be the *perfect* psychopath."

"I'm not sure if I should be flattered or concerned," I say with a shake of my head while putting my license away.

"You should be showing me to your bike, Saxon Cole," Isobel tells me as she stands and grabs my hand to pull me off my stool. "Do you have an extra helmet for me?"

"Ah, yeah, I do," I respond while following her out the door.

With another roll of her eyes, she says, "Why am I not surprised?"

CHAPTER FIVE

Isobel

Riding on the back of Sax's bike is both terrifying and exhilarating. I hold on to him, this man I don't know, for dear life, praying that he won't let me fall off the back.

Once we make it safely to the marina where he slows down and eventually comes to a complete stop in front of a row of large boats, I'm a little sad that the ride is over.

"Wow," I gasp aloud after he kills the engine and puts down the kickstand.

"Is that a good wow or a holy-shit-I'm-never-doing-that-again wow?" Sax asks over his shoulder.

"Mostly a good wow," I tell him as my fists unclench from his leather vest. "I just wasn't prepared for the amount of trust involved. At first I may have second-guessed whether or not you knew what the hell you were doing on this thing and thought I may possibly die much earlier than I expected."

Giving a grunt that sounds like he's offended, he says, "I've been riding a motorcycle for over twelve years with no fatalities so far. I don't plan to break that record anytime soon."

"Yeah, I know that now that we arrived safely," I tell him as I throw my trembling leg over to get off the dangerous machine and remove the helmet to shake out my hair. "The next time won't be nearly as scary."

"Oh really?" Sax asks. "There's gonna be a next time, huh?"

"You have to take me back to my car eventually," I point out. "And the bike is more fun than an Uber. Maybe you could even teach me how to drive one?"

"Maybe, but I'm sure as hell not teaching you on my baby. We'll have to find you a piece of shit bike to learn on," he says with a chuckle when he climbs off and removes his helmet. "Mind holding this for me while I get the bike on the boat?"

"Sure," I agree, taking it from him. "Which one of these boats is yours?"

"Guess."

"It's hard to see them clearly this late at night," I reply while glancing around. But then I spot the rugged fishing boat sitting in between two beautiful, pristine yachts. "That one?" I ask, pointing in its direction.

"That would be it," Sax says with a grin as he starts pushing the bike in that direction. He pauses before we get there and asks, "You're not allergic to cats, are you?"

"Cats?" I repeat since that's the last question I expected from him.

"Well, it's just one cat, singular. I fed a stray a few months ago, and now he doesn't seem inclined to leave my boat."

"I'm fine with cats," I assure him, thinking it's sort of adorable that a tough biker like him would have taken in a stray.

It takes Sax a few minutes to get his ramp down to push his bike on board, and then strap it onto some sort of device intended to keep it upright when the boat is moving. Once he maneuvers a cover down over it, he pulls up the anchor and I follow him inside a little room where he cranks up the engine, and then we're heading out to sea.

While we're making waves, I step out and prop my forearms on the rail to watch the lights from the marina disappear as we ride into the dark horizon that seems to go on forever. The light mist of the water hits my face like a gentle rain.

Something eventually tickles my bare ankles; and when I glance down, there's a scruffy, calico cat rubbing against me.

"Well, hello, kitty," I say, leaning down to pet its head. When he or she tips its head up at me, the moonlight glistens over one eye, while in the spot where the other eye should be is nothing but a rough patch of fur.

"Poor thing. What happened to you?"

"Not sure, but I'm guessing a cat fight," Sax says when he steps out of the room with all the buttons, gadgets and wheel.

Now I realize we've slowed to a stop and he must have killed the engine. You can no longer see the shore even in the distance. We're just floating along in the Atlantic Ocean.

"It feels like we're the only ones in the universe out here," I tell Sax after he tosses the anchor down into the water where it lands with a plop, before coming to stand beside me.

"It's amazing, right?" he asks.

"Yeah, it is...*Captain*," I agree, emphasizing his title with a seductive purr. "And I'm guessing that you show a lot of different women this incredible view."

"Maybe a few."

"A few," I scoff because I know he's full of shit.

"Fine. Several women have come aboard," he responds with a grin.

"I would also be willing to bet that you give them a night they'll never forget."

"Maybe so," he says. "But only one night. I don't do seconds or thirds."

"Good to know," I say, enjoying his honesty, because a one-night stand is all I'm capable of having. In fact, I have my own rule. Not only do I limit myself to just a single night with a man, but I also limit the number of orgasms. No reason to chance having the endorphins and other chemicals in my brain try to convince me I'm in love with some stranger just because he gives me pleasure.

Sax and I enjoy the serene view in a companionable silence for so long that my eyelids start to become heavy. But I'm not ready for the night to be over just yet.

"Do you think I could borrow one of your shirts to sleep in?" I turn to Sax and ask. "I'd really like to get out of these heels and this dress."

Lowering his eyes to the silver zipper running up the front, he says, "Only if I can unzip you. That has to be the sexiest fucking dress I've ever seen. It was made to make men obsess about undressing you."

"Then the pleasure is all yours, *Captain*," I tell him.

"Why, yes it is," he says when he grabs the zipper between his finger and thumb. Then, ever so slowly, he drags it down a slow inch at a time, exposing my bare flesh to the ocean breeze. Even though I'm practically naked other than a lacy black thong and heels once it's undone, Sax is a good boy and doesn't try to touch a single part of my skin, which is more than a little disappointing. He simply stands and stares at me when the leather puddles around my feet.

"Let me, uh, go find you a, ah, a shirt," Sax stammers even though he doesn't move a muscle to leave.

"Okay, thanks," I tell him.

"I'll be right back."

"Good," I say, and then he finally walks away.

While he's gone, I remove my shoes and then turn to look out at the sea again. It's such a beautiful, summer night. Perfect even. I bet the water below would feel amazing and be incredibly refreshing after a hot, sweaty day.

Sax

"HERE YOU GO," I say when I come up on the deck with a white t-shirt in my fist for Isobel even though I hate the thought of covering up her incredible, and very naked, body. "Isobel?" I call out when she's no longer standing in the spot where I left her. "Isobel?" I yell louder.

Then, I see her panties and shoes added to the puddle of her leather dress right before I hear a splash over on the left side of the deck, followed by her response. "Down here! The water feels amazing!"

"Down here?" I mutter to myself as I head over and look over the rail. Her head is bobbing above the waves, her blue hair wet and slicked back. "Wow, you're seriously skinny dipping in the ocean?" I say in surprise.

"Want to join me?" she asks, her teeth glowing in the darkness with the enormous smile spread across her face.

"Does a fish fuck in the water?" I reply since that's a hell yes.

Before all coherent thoughts flee from my mind, I hang the spare t-shirt over the side and go grab the ladder to secure it and make it easier for us to climb back up.

As soon as I've undressed down to my birthday suit, I hurdle over the side of the boat and land with a splash next to Isobel.

After I surface and swipe the salty water from my eyes, she says to me, "Now I can check off skinny dipping from my list."

When I'm able to see again, I notice all the smoky makeup has been washed free of Isobel's face, making her appear younger and innocent. She's even more stunning.

"You know, I've never actually done this before," I tell her as we both tread water underneath the stars. I can't take my eyes off of her. "Even when I'm out here alone I swim in a pair of boardshorts."

"Really?" she asks in surprise. "I thought you looked like a man who's broken a few rules in his life."

"Not as many as you would think."

"Have you ever been arrested?" she asks.

"Ah, only once, overnight. But thankfully, I was released without being officially charged," I answer honestly since her father only wanted a conversation when he threw me in a cell.

"What was it like?"

"It was pretty shitty," I tell her. "Boring, smelly, uncomfortable."

"I want to spend a night in jail," Isobel says excitedly.

"You're kidding, right?" I ask, and she shakes her head. "Why would you want to willingly go to jail?"

"Because I don't think you can truly appreciate your freedom until it's taken from you," she replies.

Chuckling because it's true, I tell her, "I've never met anyone like you before."

"You mean batshit crazy?" she jokes with a grin.

"No, I mean, you're so...free, living life to the fullest. I think I'm a little jealous."

"Why can't you be free too?" Isobel asks. "You have a boat that you could take anywhere."

"I could, but I don't," I reply. "For the past twelve years, it feels like I've been treading water, staying in one spot, just trying to keep my head above surface but never really moving forward."

"That doesn't sound like any fun."

"You know what? It's not, actually," I say truthfully. "I mean, I love the guys in the MC, and I would do anything for them. They would do the same for me, too, you know? But..."

"But there's something missing?" she guesses.

"Yeah, there is," I agree with a sigh. "How did you know?"

"Because I was doing the same thing until about a year ago – living a good life, but not great. It never really felt like *mine*, though. I was just getting up each morning and going through the motions to make someone else happy."

"Who were you trying to make happy?" I ask even though I have a pretty good idea.

"My father," she says on a heavy exhale. "When I found out he had been lying to me for years, that put an enormous wedge between us. I was pissed at him until I realized I didn't owe him or anyone else anything anymore. And at first it was scary to actually think about what *I* wanted for myself and having no freaking clue. Then, ideas started coming to me, all these places I wanted to go, things I wanted to do but was too scared to try before."

"So you made a list."

"I made a list and promised myself to try and cross off as many things off as possible," she says.

"What you're doing, it's incredibly brave, Isobel," I start. "But what do you do about paying for all these cool things you do?"

"Oh, well, my mother came from a wealthy family that made a fortune in tobacco. She was an only child. So, when she died, she left me everything. I think she would have wanted me to spend it this way, especially since she died so young."

"I'm sorry," I tell her sincerely. "When did you lose her?"

"I was just ten, so eighteen years ago."

"Jeez, that must have been hard."

"It was," she agrees. "But enough about me. You've seen my bucket list. What do you have on yours?"

"I don't have a bucket list."

"You really should. If you did have one, what would be the first thing you would write on it?" she asks.

"If I had a pen and paper right now, I would probably write down that I wanted to kiss you."

Smiling, she says, "I think I could grant that wish for you, Captain." Wrapping her arms around my neck, she brushes her damp lips over mine for the briefest kiss. Isobel doesn't swim away afterward, so I reach down and grab her hips, pulling her body against mine. Her soft, naked curves press against my hard body and feel even better than I thought it would. Her legs even wrap around my waist like it's the most natural thing in the world.

"Now, what else do you want to do?" she whispers.

"I bet you have a pretty good idea of what I'd like to do right now," I reply while stealing another kiss from her lips because my hardening cock is currently wedged between our naked bodies.

"Give me a better answer, and I'll let you put your tongue in my mouth."

"Deal," I agree since getting my tongue in her sounds really fucking good. "When I bought my boat several years ago, I wanted to travel all the way around the world," I admit.

"But you haven't?" Isobel asks.

"Nope. I've only been up and down the Atlantic Coast."

"Then you should go."

"It's not that easy," I reply before I capture her lips and let my tongue slip past her lips to stroke hers. The hot, wet contact makes my cock twitch with the need to be inside of her. When Isobel tilts her hips like she's trying to impale herself on me, I'm glad I'm not the only one overcome by desire.

"What else?" she asks. Her fingers spear through my hair and grab on tight, tilting my head back so her mouth can come down on the side of my neck, making it impossible to think clearly.

CHAPTER SIX

Isobel

I've been with my fair share of men over the last few months, making up for lost time after being celibate for the first half of my twenties, but none have had bodies as big and ripped as Sax's. If I wouldn't die of oxygen deprivation, I would gladly sink down into the depths of the ocean to kiss every single inch of him, especially the hard ones currently jutting into my lower belly.

While some guys would've already tried to slip it inside of me by now, Sax is being a patient gentleman. And I'm not ashamed to say I'm not making it easy on him by licking his neck and rubbing my slit up and down his steely length, enjoying the pleasurable friction on my clit.

"I don't know if you're trying to drown me or fuck me," Sax says, his voice huskier and deeper when he grips my ass cheek tightly in his left hand and then reaches behind me with his right to grab onto one of the rails of the ladder. The move lifts us out of the water a few inches so that the waves are no longer breaking in our face. "You said we had to keep things PG-13 tonight, but we're already in R territory."

"Good. I'm ready for R," I reply, then sit my butt on one of the rungs of the ladder so that I'm only submerged from my calves down. Sax lunges forward and licks up the drips of water from my stomach before his lips move upward and cover one of my beaded nipples.

"Oh god," I moan as I grasp both sides of his face between my hands to keep him right where he is. He applies suction and then flicks his tongue over the sensitive flesh, making me squirm on the step as I think of having his tongue someplace lower. As if reading my mind, Sax releases my nipple and kisses his way down my stomach. While his right hand keeps a grip on the ladder railing, his left covers my knee and pushes it to the side, opening me up to him.

Glancing up at my face with desire filling his eyes, his tongue swipes over my damp pelvis, before he says, "I'm gonna lick your pussy until your legs shake, unless you have any objections?"

"Nope. No objections," I pant thanks to my racing pulse and rapid breathing caused by the anticipation.

Sax swipes his index finger right through my folds, and then his face leans forward so his tongue can take the same path.

"Oh holy shit!" I exclaim as his finger penetrates me just as a wave splashes up right between my legs. My hands shoot out to grab on to the ladder rails to hang on for dear life as his mouth gets in on the action, his tongue working overtime as it circles and flicks and fucks me into oblivion.

"Oh god. *Oh god!*" I scream as my eyes slam shut. My back arches and my hips buck, needing more. There are so many amazing sensations I can't keep up with them all – the cool ocean breeze over my bare breasts, the waves slapping me between my legs while Sax's finger pumps inside of me and his tongue... "Right there! Yes! Yes! *Yesss!*" I shout at the top of my lungs when my thighs tremble and my entire body convulses. It's one of the few times I don't panic when either of those things happen to me. These are the pleasurable shudders that are so intense and feel so good they nearly hurt.

When I finally stop shaking, I let go of the rails and sink down into the water again. Or I'm being pulled, I'm not sure which. It doesn't matter, because Sax is there, holding me in his strong grip. I wrap my legs around his waist, and then my back is pressed against the ladder rungs as the blunt head of his hard cock drives inside of me. There's no resistance. My body accepts all of him, letting him fill me up until he hits the bullseye that makes me cry out his name. My nails dig into his back, hanging on for dear life as Sax uses all of his strength to pump in and out of me, jarring my teeth with his powerful thrusts as if he's trying to get deeper with each one. Sounds I've never made before escape from my throat and echo around us in the darkness.

"God, Isobel," Sax groans into the side of my neck. "You've got me. So. Fucking. Hot. The way you taste, the sound of your screams. You're so goddamn beautiful, I had to get inside of you."

"Yes! Don't stop," I beg him as his hips move faster. My own are eager to try and keep up as the pleasure builds and builds from the spot he's hitting inside me and the way my clit grinds against his pelvis. Just when I think Sax can't feel any better, he slams his cock as deep as it will go.

"Work your pussy on my cock until you come on it," he orders before his mouth returns to mine. Our tongues battle each other as I do as he wanted, not that I really have a choice in the matter. My body is frantic for the relief it can only get from the rock-hard inches currently impaling me. Later, I may even be embarrassed by how aggressively I humped him, but now all I can focus on is chasing the pleasure.

"Fuck me, harder, baby. There you go," Sax says when I break our kiss to throw my head back and slam my hips down on him over and over again. "Look at me while you get yourself off."

I blink my heavy eyelids open and meet his while I keep riding his cock.

"Do you like how I feel?" he asks.

"Yes," I answer.

"You want to come so bad, don't you?"

"So bad!" I agree with a vigorous nod of my head.

"Show me how you rub your needy little clit when you're horny and there's no tongue to lick it for you."

I slip my right hand from his shoulder and slide it down my stomach until I get to the water just above where our bodies are joined. The whole time my gaze is locked on Sax's piercing blue eyes. I gasp when my fingertips touch just the right spot.

"My tongue remembers that spot," Sax says. "That's how I'm going to wake you up in the morning. I'm gonna bury my face between your legs and eat your pussy until it's dripping wet."

"*Yes*," I moan as I remember every second of his talented mouth working me over.

"Then I'm going to put you on your hands and knees and give you my cock. After I unload deep inside of you, you're gonna thank me for the wake-up pussy licking by sucking me clean until I explode down your throat."

"Oh, fuck!" I gasp as I get closer and closer.

"I want you swallowing my cum while it's still seeping down your thighs."

"Oh my god," I moan from his dirty talk that's so filthy I could probably get off with it on its own. With his cock buried inside me and my fingers playing with my clit, I blast off into orgasm heaven where my limbs go limp from the intensity of the pleasure coursing through my veins.

I vaguely remember Sax moving inside of me again, fucking me with several hard, fast thrusts before he growls out a curse next to my ear.

Sex will never be this good with anyone else is the first rational thought in my lust-hazed mind.

~

Sax

"I'M SORRY. We shouldn't – I shouldn't have done that," I tell Isobel as soon as the blood returns to my head where it needs to be to avoid making stupid fucking decisions like this.

"It's okay. I'm glad you did," she assures me, her lips brushing over my damp shoulder.

No, she wouldn't say that if she knew the truth.

"You said to keep it PG-13," I remind her.

"That was before I got naked with you in the ocean," Isobel says. "I thought that was a pretty obvious signal that I wanted you."

"Still...I should've used a condom. I *always* wear condoms," I say, unable to tell her the real reason I feel guilty for screwing her.

"I'm clean and you can't get me pregnant, if that's what you're worried about."

"You're on birth control?" I ask, even though the question is a little late.

"No," she replies. "Even better, I've had my tubes tied."

"Really?" I ask with my brow furrowed, the confusion temporarily pushing the guilt aside. "Why did you do that? You're so young. You don't want to have any children?"

"Definitely not any of my own," she responds.

"Why not?" I ask, unable to let it go because it doesn't make sense. I don't understand why she would go into pediatric nursing if she doesn't like kids.

"For shitty reasons I would rather not dwell on today when the night is so perfect and we're swimming naked in the middle of the Atlantic Ocean."

"Fair enough," I agree.

"I've already came twice for you, so just so you know, even though it was amazing, and I would love to take you up on that promise for tomorrow morning, I can only be with you one more time at most," Isobel informs me. Forget confused and guilty. Now I'm filled with disappointment.

"We can only fuck one more time?" I repeat. "You mean one more time tonight or forever?" I ask since I was planning to be inside of her at least twice more before I wake her up with my tongue between her legs tomorrow.

"Forever," Isobel responds, which is discouraging, not just because of my assignment but because I already know that three times with her could never be enough. "It's a bucket list thing," she adds. "No getting attached or falling in love, so no more than three orgasms with the same man. Besides, you said you only do one-night stands anyway."

"Why exactly is three orgasms the magic number? I thought the more the merrier," I question her, hoping that I can figure out some sort of loop hole to get around her rule.

"Well, after three orgasms, all of those happy endorphins in a woman's brain start making her trust and bond to the guy. And in men, the dopamine released after a release causes intense pleasure, obviously, which can cause them to form an addiction to one woman. A couple may think they're developing feelings for each other when it's really just chemistry caused by sex."

"And all that's bad because..." I ask, noticing that she sounds like a nurse even if she's pretending she's not one.

"Because I don't have time to get tied down to anyone," she replies.

"Oh," I mutter when it becomes clear that getting her to stay with me for more than a night is going to be even harder than I imagined. "If I had known about your rule before, I would've made your first two times even better. Can I get a do over?" I ask, only half joking.

"It would've been impossible to make the first two times any better," Isobel says with a smile.

"Yeah? I sort of thought so too," I agree. Brushing her wet hair out of her face and behind her ear, I tell her, "I wouldn't change anything about tonight, especially meeting you. You look like you belong here with me, swimming naked in the ocean under a starry sky – a mermaid in her natural habitat."

"A mermaid?" she scoffs and then laughs almost as lovely as she sings.

"Or I guess I should've said siren," I amend.

"Wow. Never heard either of those before. I'll give you credit for originality in your attempted pick up line compliments, even though it's a moot point since you've already gotten laid."

"Yeah, but I want to get laid by you again, at least one more time," I tell her. "And I meant every word. You're mesmerizing in the moonlight."

"It is so nice being out here, away from civilization. Thank you again for bringing me."

"Thank you for agreeing to come aboard the boat of a possible serial killer."

"I'm all about taking chances nowadays. I blame my father for making me play it safe for so long it nearly made me go insane."

"So I guess I have him to thank for the amazing fuck," I say. "I'll be sure to mention it at his birthday dinner tomorrow night."

"Please do!" she agrees with a bark of laughter. "That would be hilarious. And, um, did I mention to you that he lives in Raleigh?"

"Ah, no, you didn't," I reply, even though I had an idea. "We're driving to Raleigh tomorrow night?"

"Do you mind?" she asks while biting her bottom lip in concern.

"After skinny dipping and fucking you out here, I would gladly drive us to California tomorrow if you asked me to."

"Thanks, even though that would be impossible," she responds with a kiss on my lips. When she pulls away, her finger trails down my chest and below the water where Willy's scratches are starting to heal up underneath my chain necklace. "So, ah, what exactly happened here? Wild night of sex?"

"No, definitely not," I grumble. "You remember that cat I told you about?"

"I've met her."

"Her? I thought it was a he. Anyway, Willy can be a little jumpy when he hears strange noises at night," I explain.

"She sleeps on top of you?"

"No matter how many times I run him off," I reply. "Or her."

"A cat that knows what she wants. I just hope she won't attack me when I join you in bed."

"Don't worry. I won't let that happen," I promise. "You ready to head back up?" I ask.

"I guess so. I am pretty exhausted," Isobel replies with a sigh.

"You're welcome," I joke.

CHAPTER SEVEN

Isobel

"Why isn't it that easy?" I ask Sax as we settle into his bed on our sides, facing each other under the sheets with the bedside lamp on. All I'm wearing is one of his shirts and he just has on a pair of gray boxer briefs. Before his head hits the pillow, his one-eyed cat came scampering up on his side where it wasted no time flopping down on top of its owner as if laying claim to him in case I was getting any ideas about that final round of sex. I swear her face even looks smug as her lips curl up and she closes her one good eye.

Message received, kitty, I think to myself as I reach up to scratch her behind her ears.

"What do you mean? What's not easy?" Sax responds. His fingers slip under the hem of my shirt; but instead of touching me in a naughty way, they come to a rest on my hipbone where the pad of his thumb starts to rub circles.

"When I said you should travel the world on your boat, you said it wasn't that easy. Why not?"

"Oh," he mutters. "Well, the MC is basically a lifelong commitment. And since I'm an officer, I can't just come and go when I want."

"That sounds depressing," I tell him.

"It's not so bad," Sax replies, his thumb still caressing my hip. "I knew what I was getting myself into when I earned my patch. And the guys are great. They took a chance on me, so the least I can do is help them out as much as I can."

"You say that like you think you owe them your life."

"In a way I do," he says. "And the business side of things is good. I make decent money that I couldn't make anywhere else with half a bachelor's degree in archaeology."

"You dropped out of school?"

"In my sophomore year, yeah," he says.

"Why?"

"Because the girl I was hoping to one day marry died from a drug overdose."

"Oh wow, Sax," I gasp in surprise. "That must have been really hard on you."

"It was," he says. "April was seeing other people at the time, but I was young, foolish, and in love with her. I was certain she would eventually come back to me after she finished her last year of high school, so we were doing the long-distance thing," he tells me. "I blamed myself. Hell, I still blame myself for not being there to watch out for her."

"You shouldn't. Everyone makes their own decisions. Even if you had been there, you probably wouldn't have been able to help her," I tell him.

My eyes lower to the chain hanging around his neck that I first noticed in the water when he was naked, and more specifically the dainty, white gold ring with a sapphire heart surrounded by tiny diamonds hanging from it that obviously belonged to a woman.

"Was this hers?" I ask, tapping the ring with my fingernail.

"Ah, yeah, it was," Sax responds, removing his hand from my hip to wrap his fingers around it. "How is it that I just met you hours ago and you're already unlocking all of my deep, dark secrets?" he jokes with a smile that doesn't reach his eyes. "And it's getting late. The sun will be up soon, so we should probably get some sleep. We've got a long ride to Raleigh tomorrow."

"Okay, Captain," I agree even though I want to know more about him and his past. I get the feeling that Sax just realized he's told me much more about himself than he wanted to. But I like how he's opening up to me, telling me things that I'm guessing not many people, if any, know about him. Talking to him is so easy and natural, like we've known each other for years, not just hours. I would love to spend more time with him, to get to know him better, but I have to keep moving. At least we'll have one more day together before I get back on the road. Besides, any man who still wears another woman's jewelry clearly isn't over her yet.

"I'm glad I met you tonight," Sax says, then brushes his lips over my cheek.

"Me too," I agree. "Goodnight, Sax."

"Night," he replies, then reaches behind him to turn off the lamp. Kitty just hunkers down on his side as her owner moves, refusing to abandon her position. And I can't say that I blame her.

CHAPTER EIGHT

Sax

"Y ou failed to mention that your family was filthy rich," I say to Isobel over my shoulder after killing the engine on my bike in front of the three-story brick mansion. The entire ride over my mind has been racing, trying to come up with a way to keep her around.

"There's, ah, one other thing I probably should have mentioned too," Isobel says while climbing off the back of my Harley.

"Oh yeah? What's that?" I ask even though I have a pretty damn good idea.

Her fingers fidget with the strap of her crossbody purse. "This isn't really my house. It's actually the governor's mansion. What I mean is my father *is* the, ah, current governor."

"No shit?" I ask, removing my helmet so that I don't have to look at her and lie right to her face about the fact I already knew that. "Lawrence Washington is your father?"

"He is," she answers. "And he's a major dick with more power than any one man should have."

"Should I be worried about him tossing me in a dungeon and throwing away the key just for sleeping with his daughter?" I joke.

"No, he's not that insane. I don't think," she replies. "Come on, let's get this over with."

Once I'm off the bike, I hang my helmet on the handlebar and Isobel takes my hand, leading me up the walkway to the stairs at the front of the house. The door opens before we reach it, revealing the goofy guy from the bar.

"Hey, it's you!" I say. He starts to shut the door in our faces before I throw a hand out to stop him.

"Stu still hasn't forgotten your knife," Isobel whispers just as her father, dressed down in dark slacks and a white button-down, pushes his minion aside.

"Isobel!" he says in greeting, a smile lighting up his face before saying, "You actually came! And you're wearing leather. Is your hair...blue?"

"It's turquoise with purple highlights," she corrects him as they stand and face each other awkwardly. "No one would ever suspect I'm the governor's daughter in this disguise, would they?" she asks, then points a finger at the center of his chest and says, "And I told you to stop sending people to *fetch* me for you like I'm a child or a dog."

"I didn't think you would come otherwise, and I've missed you," her father says before his gaze finally lands on me and he does a double take. "But I'm glad you're here and that you brought a guest."

"Dad, this is Sax. Sax, this is my father, Lawrence Washington."

"'Sup?" I say, taking Isobel's hand in my right one to avoid shaking the scumbag's hand.

"I wish we would've known you were bringing your...friend to dinner," her father says, his eyes lowered and narrowed at my hand on hers.

"Sax is my boyfriend. We're in love and who knows, we may elope and get married one day," she lies to him.

"I highly doubt that," her dad mutters.

Too bad he knows she's lying because he coerced me to lie to her before we ever met. God, I keep sinking deeper and deeper into this shit. Remembering how many people's lives are depending on me pulling this off helps soothe my conscious for screwing over a nice girl like Isobel, at least temporarily.

"Well, come in I guess," her father says. Once Isobel and I clear the doorway, he must spot my bike out front. "You brought my daughter here on that death trap?" he exclaims.

"My bike is one of the many things she loves about me, isn't that right, baby?" I ask Isobel whose hand is still clasped in mine.

"Oh yeah. Harleys are so hot," she replies. "I still can't believe they go that fast! It felt like we were flying!"

The color drains from her father's face as he digests that lie. I wouldn't be racing around, driving like a maniac with Isobel on the back of my bike. But I don't mind letting him think I'm that careless. It's his own fault for putting her in this position with me where I could easily endanger her life.

"If anything happens to her, I'll hunt you down," he warns me under his breath.

"Dad, stop," Isobel says. "That's no way to talk to our guest and your future son-in-law."

Sighing heavily with exasperation, he says, "Dinner is on the table in the dining room. Why don't we head on in there? Unless you two need to clean up first?" he asks, basically implying that I'm a dirty pile of trash that's underneath him. He knew what I was *before* he insisted that I meet his daughter.

"I should probably go wash up," I agree. Winking at the governor, I say, "You don't even want to know all the naughty places my hands have been."

He growls an indecipherable curse before Isobel drags me down the hall and away from him. She pulls me into a fancy bathroom with lace on the hand towels and even a chandelier hanging from the ceiling. What a way to spend taxpayer dollars.

"Jeez, he hates you already," Isobel whispers gleefully with a broad smile while she presses her back against the door. Then, her hands are grabbing at the front of my jeans, pulling me closer and fumbling with the button and zipper.

"What are you doing?" I ask her, even though it seems pretty obvious.

"I want you to fuck my mouth in this pretentious house," she says as she jerks my undone jeans and boxer briefs down my thighs. "Besides, I still owe you an orgasm to make things even between us."

Fuck, I want her mouth but don't want it to be our last time. I *can't* let it be the last time since amazing sex is all I have up my sleeve to convince her to stick around after dinner.

"I don't know if now is really the time or place, Iz," I whisper, my head so fucked up that my dick was completely flaccid until her fingers wrap around it. All the blood in my body rushes south so fast I sway from the sudden onset of dizziness.

"I'll make it worth your while, Captain. Promise," Isobel says, as if I had any doubts about her skills before she sinks down to her knees. Keeping her eyes lifted to my face the entire time, she guides the head of my shaft in between her parted lips.

"Oh shit, woman," I gasp as her wet tongue licks my slit and then coats the underside of my cock. I have to slap my right palm on the door above her to catch myself when my knees go weak. Once I've braced myself, my hips start pumping involuntarily, thrusting my dick deeper into her mouth until her nose is finally pressed against my pelvis.

"Goddamn that's good," I groan as my left-hand cups the back of her head to hold her still so I can fuck her mouth like she wanted.

It feels so amazing I don't ever want her to stop sucking my dick, especially since this could be the last time we fool around. But I can only last so long before I erupt down her throat. She takes everything I give her too, without even a grunt of complaint.

As soon as she releases my cock from her mouth to wipe the corners of her lips, I grab her shoulders to pull her to her feet. Holding her face between my hands, I cover her lips with mine, not minding tasting myself on her. "Thanks for that," I tell her as I lower my hands down her sides and around to cup her ass cheeks under her leather dress. Hoping that she got herself worked up sucking me off, I say, "Let me take care of you too."

"No, that's okay," Isobel says, taking a step back and removing my hands from her body. "We, um, better get back out there. If we're gone much longer, he may break the door down to get in here."

"Okay, but you're going to stay with me again tonight, right?" I ask while pulling up my pants. As soon as the question leaves my mouth, I can tell by the surprised look on her face that she hadn't planned to stay with me on my boat again. "I thought we had fun last night," I say to try and convince her to come home with me, not just as a job for her father but because I want her back in my bed, more than any other woman since the one I lost twelve years ago.

"Yeah, last night was fun, but you know my bucket list rule."

"We haven't been together three times yet," I remind her.

"Three orgasms is the limit, not the minimum requirement," she says without meeting my eyes. Fuck, I'm already losing her, and it hasn't even been twenty-four hours. There has to be something I can do to convince her to stick around.

"I know a tattoo artist," I blurt out when I suddenly remember seeing the entry on her bucket list. "Gabriel Cross is an amazing artist who can draw anything you want, and he's a Savage King. If I call him, he could probably squeeze you in tomorrow morning."

"We'll see," she says before she turns and walks out of the bathroom. Her answer isn't a no, but it sounds like I have my work cut out for me to make it turn into a yes.

My shoulders are already slumped when I wash up and go search for the dining room. I'm feeling disappointed even after the amazing head she gave me because Isobel's ready to bolt on me. But seeing another dude's arms around her sends a punch of adrenaline right through my system.

"Who the hell is he?" I ask, not missing the smirk on her father's face from where he's sitting at the head of a long ass table that seats around sixteen people.

"Oh, Sax, this is my friend Daniel I told you about. Daniel this is my...boyfriend Sax," Isobel says when she slips out of his arms.

The fucker with his plaid shirt tucked into his tight white pants glances over and gives me a look that says he's sizing me up. "Well, Izzie, that's one way to piss off your father," he mutters.

I just met him, and I already hate him, mostly because he had his hands on Isobel, but also because he's right. I could never deserve a good girl like her, and she would never have brought me here for anything other than a big "fuck you" to her father.

And why is this rage-filled jealousy trying to claw its way up out of my throat when we're not really together? I shouldn't give a shit who touches Isobel as long as she stays in town and makes amends with her father. But I do care.

"You haven't told him we're eloping yet?" I ask Isobel when she comes around to the other side of the table where I'm standing.

"No, Danny, um, just got here," she says, placing a kiss on my cheek.

"No way Izzie would get married and not invite me," the dick says with a grin. "Besides, I'm guessing you two just met since you sent me his driver's license photo *last night*."

Without responding to that statement calling her bluff, Isobel says, "Let's all have a seat and dig in."

She pulls out the chair closest to the end of the table near her father, so I take the one beside her. On the opposite side, Daniel lowers himself into a chair. Guess he's joining us for dinner.

Silently, Isobel passes me a bowl filled with salad, while other dishes get passed around the table. It actually looks damn good, so I pick up my fork and stab a carrot. As soon as it's in my mouth, dickhead Daniel says, "Shouldn't we say grace before we eat?"

"By all means," I agree with my mouth full before chewing it up.

He bows his head and closes his eyes, with Isobel and her father following suit.

"Heavenly Father, we thank you for the nutritious food you've put on our table and for blessing us with your glory as we celebrate Lawrence's birthday tonight. Help guide us back down the path of righteousness, even when we make a wrong turn. In your name we pray. Amen."

Why do I get the feeling he's referring to me as Isobel's "wrong turn"?

"Amen," her father says. "Thank you, Daniel. I'm so glad you could join us to celebrate my birthday."

"Me too," Isobel agrees with a smile.

"So where have you been lately, Izzie? I haven't seen your Instagram in a few months to keep up with all of your recent bucket list accomplishments."

Yeah, right. He's got cyber-stalker written all over his face.

And it doesn't take a genius to see that the governor would love for his daughter to end up with someone like Daniel, who is obviously from a wealthy family. I think Isobel said his father is police chief, so that connection would be beneficial to him too. But I guess he wasn't the man for her and didn't give her a reason to stick around.

"Well," Isobel starts, her face lighting up as she starts ticking items off on her fingers. "I finally climbed the Statue of Liberty, went rafting through the Grand Canyon. I've seen the secret city of Machu Picchu, Peru, snorkeled with endangered leatherback sea turtles in Barbados, walked along the Great Wall of China, visited the pyramids in Giza, drank a glass of wine under the Eiffel Tower, and went on an African safari!"

"Wow, that's pretty impressive," Daniel says, echoing my thoughts. She wasn't kidding about wanting to see the world. "I would've loved to tag along. Where did you meet him? On some mountain top?" he asks snidely, nodding in my direction.

"Ah, no. Sax and I only met recently," she replies, glancing over at me and leaving out the part about the bar. "Love at first sight and all that."

"Right. Yeah," Daniel says, sounding unconvinced.

"So, he's going to be accompanying you from now on?" her father asks.

"Ah, well, we haven't decided what we're going to do next," Isobel tells him, clearly not wanting to come right out and lie to her father with everyone else at the table, even though she has no problem pretending to be in love with me. Or is it that she doesn't want to lie to me, knowing I won't be around on her next great adventure?

"We're happy to just take it one day at a time, aren't we?" I say, covering Isobel's hand with mine.

"Impulsiveness is often a symptom..." Daniel starts, causing Isobel to glare at him. Is he implying that she would have to be crazy to want a guy like me? He's probably right.

"I'm not being impulsive. I'm just living my life to the fullest," she responds through clenched teeth.

Her father clears his throat between bites, and then asks, "So what exactly do you do for a living...Sax?"

"I'm an officer in an MC, a motorcycle club, that owns many lucrative businesses. Each member gets a cut every quarter," I explain, even though he already knows.

"*Legal* businesses?" Daniel questions.

"Sure, mostly," I answer with a smirk.

Under the table, Isobel gives my thigh a squeeze and says, "Daniel's father is the police chief in Cary," as if she's worried that I'll say something to get myself in trouble. She has no fucking idea how much trouble I'm in. And it's not like I can just come out and tell her that me and the majority of the other guys in the MC were caught killing twenty men by her father, then ask if she could please go back to being a good girl for a few more months to help us avoid life sentences.

"What do your business ventures entail?" Danny-boy asks.

"A hotel, strip club, tattoo studio and bar all in Emerald Isle. Tourism on the coast is always growing," I tell him. "So what do you do, Daniel?" I ask.

"Didn't Isobel tell you?" he responds, flashing a mega-watt, douchey smile in her direction. "I have my own pediatric practice."

Great, he's a fucking doctor. If I had to guess, I bet Isobel was a nurse at his facility. It's just a match made in heaven, yet Isobel must not care about him if she's been traveling the world on her own. I get it. He's too...conservative for a girl who says she loves spontaneity. Anything other than missionary in the bedroom is probably more than the rich prick can handle.

So no, I'm not jealous of the relationship old Danny has with Isobel. I'm just not a fan of the way he looks at her, like she's the one that got away and he hasn't given up hope on getting her back.

My theory about how he feels about her is confirmed when Daniel goes on to say, "A kid could be screaming their lungs out because they were scared or suffering, and all Isobel had to do was sing "Walking on Sunshine" to them and they would instantly calm down. The kids just adored her and so did their parents."

"Not all of the parents," Isobel mutters quietly.

"Oh, it's not just kids. Isobel has that effect on everyone," I say honestly as I slip my arm around her back. "I started falling for her the first time I heard her sing too."

Game on, jackass.

CHAPTER NINE

Isobel

"What are you doing with that loser, Izzie?" Daniel whispers when Sax excuses himself after dinner and steps outside to make a phone call.

"He's not a loser," I huff as I start clearing the table. My father was the first to vanish, disappearing to attend to business, of course. Forget that it's his birthday or that I rarely visit. He has a state to run and decisions to make.

"If you say so," Daniel mutters, gathering up the drinking glasses.

"Jeez, Danny, just because someone isn't rich or didn't go to medical school like you doesn't mean they have any less worth as a human being," I say as I head for the kitchen with Daniel following me.

"Hey now, he's the one calling himself a 'Savage King,' not me. The word *savage* says it all, don't you think? Those guys are violent and ruthless."

"I may not have known Sax for long, but he's neither of those things," I respond as I place the dishes in the sink and take the glasses from Daniel's hands. "All I know is that I like him. He's...fun."

"You can do better, Izzie. You *deserve* better. The guy runs with a bad crew."

"I appreciate your concern, but it's unnecessary," I tell him. "You sound like my father, by the way. You two have been spending way too much time together."

Laying his hand on my arm, Daniel says, "We're just worried about you. We both thought you needed a few weeks to come to terms with everything, but it's been a year now. When are you going to stop this craziness?"

"You of all people should know that I only have a few good years left. I don't intend to waste them," I remind him.

"So then ditch the biker and let me come with you," Daniel pleads.

"You have a practice to run," I point out, rather than tell him the truth – that I don't want him tagging along, reporting everything I do back to my father.

"My associates can cover for me," he says.

"Daniel, I'm sorry, but you should stay here."

"You shouldn't be alone, Izzie, especially when you don't know when your symptoms may worsen! What if you're driving and have a wreck? You need someone looking out for you."

"I'll turn in my license before it gets that bad," I assure him. "And I have Sax," I lie, since tonight will be the last time I see the hot biker before I hit the road.

"And who is going to look out for you with him?" Daniel grumbles through clenched teeth.

"Stop worrying about me. I'm not a child, despite the fact that you and my father still treat me like one."

"We care about you and don't want you to end up dead on the side of the road somewhere," he replies.

"Maybe that's what you worry about. My father is just

concerned that the media will catch me doing something he doesn't like and that it'll hurt his numbers at the polls."

"You know there's more to him than that," Daniel says.

"I'm not so sure."

"Just, promise me you'll be careful," he says. "And if you need anything, call me. I'll come to you even if you're halfway across the world."

"I know you would," I reply with a small smile. "Thanks, Danny," I say when I give him a hug.

"You ready to hit the road?" Sax asks from the doorway of the kitchen, his voice deeper and more commanding than I've ever heard it.

"Yeah, just saying goodbye," I say as I pull away from Daniel.

"Take care of yourself," he says, kissing my cheek before he lets me go.

And, for the first time since last night when we met in the parking lot, I see an inclination toward violence on Sax's handsome, normally cheerful face. Not that he looks like he would hurt me, but Daniel probably shouldn't ever be alone with him for any period of time.

"Everything okay?" I ask Sax when I take his hand to pull him toward the mansion's front door. There's no reason to even seek out my father, who is likely occupied with business. Besides, we've already said our goodbyes after dinner.

"You know he wants you, right?" Sax grits out when we're facing each other beside his bike in the darkness, only the interior lights of the house providing a soft glow on the yard.

"Why do you care?" I ask. Going up on my toes to whisper in his ear, I grasp the front of his cut in both of my fists for balance and say, "You're just pretending to be my boyfriend, remember?"

"What if we stop pretending?" Sax asks, placing his hands on my hips. "You could stay here..."

"Oh, god," I groan, and playfully press my palms to his chest push him away. "Now you're starting to sound like those two!" I say as I point my index finger back at the house. "I'm not staying *anywhere* until I cross off every single item on my bucket list."

"That could take years," he says.

"You could start working on your own list," I suggest. "Traveling around the world will take a while too."

"I can't," Sax says with a sigh.

"That's too bad," I mutter. "You should follow your heart and do whatever you want to do before it's too late. But either way, I guess our time together is coming to an end."

"Not yet. I have something planned, something you can cross off tonight before getting your tattoo tomorrow."

"I'll think about it on the ride back," I tell him.

"You do that," he says, grabbing the helmet and placing it on my head to fasten the chin strap. "And I'll think about how I'm not taking you back to your car just yet," Sax says with a grin before he throws a leg over his bike. And I have to admit he looks mighty good straddling the Harley. His hands gripping the handlebars cause the muscles in his thick arms to flex in the glow from the house. "Are you staying with your pops or taking your chances with me?" he asks when I stand there staring at him. He thinks I'm being indecisive when really, I was just ogling him.

Climbing up behind him, my thighs hug his hips as I situate my feet on the pegs and then wind my arms around Sax's waist to hold on tight.

"I guess I'm your prisoner," I joke with a smile as he pulls on his helmet.

"Oh, you have no idea," he responds with a chuckle before he cranks the engine.

ON THE TWO and a half hour ride back from to the coast, I try to decide if I'm going to stay with Sax tonight after whatever he has planned, or if I should just get into my car and hit the road, heading up to my next stop, which is Charlotte for a bar gig the day after tomorrow before catching a flight to the United Kingdom to get to Bristol before the International Balloon Fiesta.

Part of me wants nothing more than to join Sax on his boat again, sail it out into the ocean and forget the rest of the world exists for a while.

And that's the part that scares me the most, because I can't let myself get so attached to him that leaving tomorrow is impossible.

On the other hand, he did promise me a tattoo from an amazing artist...

Sure, I could find someone else to ink my cherry blossoms, but how would I know if they're any good? Sax has a monster of a tattoo on his back, the Savage King MC skull king logo and words, so I trust his judgment on such things.

I'm starting to realize I trust him more than I should for a man I haven't known very long. Damn those orgasm endorphins!

I have to say that after placing my trust in him, the last place I expected him to take me when we got back to the coast is the Carteret County Sheriff's Department.

As soon as Sax kills the engine, we both climb off and remove our helmets, eager to get the sensation back in our legs. Then, I turn to him and ask, "Are you stopping here to ask for directions?"

"Not exactly," he responds and then his lips are on mine and his hands are pulling me closer, exploring my curves. Moving his mouth down my neck to lick and suck, stealing my breath, he tells me, "You have no idea how many times I almost pulled over to get inside of you. Having your legs around me for that long, while not being able to touch you was torture."

"Sorry?" I gasp as his hands slip up the outsides of my thighs, heading under my dress to squeeze my ass cheeks. I'm so distracted that I don't notice anyone approaching us.

At least not until a woman's voice says from behind me, "Saxon Cole and Isobel Washington, you're both under arrest for, eh, indecent exposure."

Sax lifts his mouth from my neck, then tells the unknown woman, "If you think this is indecent, then you should've been there when we were skinny dipping in the ocean last night."

"I'll have to take your word for it," she says on a sigh.

Removing his palms from under my skirt, Sax reaches down to grab my hands and place them both at the small of my back. "Cuff her, Sheriff. I've already frisked her for you."

My eyes widen and my jaw drops when the metal snaps tightly over each of my wrists. "*This* was what you had planned?" I ask Sax.

"You're the crazy woman who has *spend a night in jail* on her bucket list," he says with a chuckle.

Spinning around to face the woman who is conducting my fake arrest, I tell her, "Don't go easy on me."

"Whatever you say," the young, pretty brunette snorts. "Are you going into the cell with her?" she asks Sax.

"Yep," he answers.

"Come on, then. If this is some weird kink, I don't even want to know," she tells us with a chuckle.

"Like you and your husband never break out the cuffs in the bedroom," Sax says, and I swear the sheriff's cheeks redden.

CHAPTER TEN

Sax

Being locked up with Isobel is much more fun than when her father locked me up alone.

"So, is being arrested everything you thought it would be?" I ask her as I pull her down onto my lap, sitting her sideways since I'm taking up the single metal chair. There are two beds, but the floor looks more comfortable.

"It smells worse than I imagined," she says with her nose wrinkled up adorably.

"No shit," I agree with a grunt.

"And it's so loud," she adds, obviously referring to the man chanting "*Give me freedom, or give me death!*" over and over again, the words echoing off the concrete walls. Fisting the front of my cut, she brushes her lips over mine and says, "But I'm glad you're here with me. I doubt it would be as much fun alone."

"Anything to keep you around a little longer," I tell her sincerely.

She seems so set on leaving me already, and I've realized that I don't just want her to stay because of her father. I really adore this woman.

"Well, I have been thinking about that tattoo tomorrow," she replies while biting down on her bottom lip.

"Oh, yeah?" I ask in surprise. I half expected her to give me the same spiel about having to keep moving as soon as we're released from our cell in the morning.

"If your artist friend is available, then I would like for him to ink me."

"Any ideas on what you want Gabe to design and where you'll put it?" I ask her, relieved and excited about her staying in town a little longer. Now I just need to figure out some reason to convince her to stay longer – as in months – and go back into nursing.

"I was thinking of a cherry blossom that starts here," Isobel says pointing to the spot right below her hipbone. "And ends about here, with a lifelike butterfly sitting on it." Her finger trails down her upper thigh and I can just picture the pink flowers inked right along-side her sweet little pussy. I'm not a huge fan of having another man doing the job, though. If it has to be someone, at least it will be Gabe. I completely trust him to not just to do a killer design, but to keep his eyes and hands to himself. It doesn't hurt that I know about his secret conjugal visits with Ian...

"What do you think?" Isobel asks, glancing over her shoulder to see my reaction.

"I bet it'll look amazing," I tell her truthfully before I grab her face to turn it toward me so I can kiss her lips.

"Now, how would you feel about adding *have sex in a jail cell* to your bucket list?" I suggest.

"Sounds good to me," she whispers.

"From what I hear, it can get pretty dirty," I warn her.

"I can take it."

"Can you?" I ask.

"Oh yeah," she agrees. "But then this is it. No more sex for us. No more orgasms."

"I guess we better make it count," I tell her before I grab the back of her neck to tip her backward and kiss her. Isobel grips my shoulders hard as if she's afraid I would let her fall. She's right not to trust me, but I've got her right now. She isn't going anywhere unless I want her to.

"I have you," I say against her lips before I deepen our kiss. I feel the moment her body relaxes, giving herself over to me. I could do anything I wanted to her and she would let me. It's wrong for me to take advantage of her, but I can't seem to resist putting my hands on her, kissing her, being inside of her.

And while she may claim this will be the last time we're together, I think she'll make an exception to her three orgasms per man rule. She has to. Everything is riding on me convincing her to stay and go back to being her father's perfect daughter again.

For now, all I want is to worship her body. Hopefully, I'll give it to her so good that she'll keep wanting more.

Isobel

BEING WITH SAX IS DANGEROUS. He makes me feel too much when I'm supposed to be keeping things between us physical without any emotions.

But he looks at me like I'm more than an extended one-night stand. And when he kisses me, I can't help it, I melt.

So enough with his deep, soulful kisses. It'll be hard to keep our mouths on each other if I'm riding him. When I remove my lips from his, Sax pulls me back up and I'm able to throw my leg over his to straddle him.

"Mmm," I say as I look down between my legs and see the bulge in his jeans. "You're nice and hard already."

"I think just seeing you is enough to make my dick swell," Sax responds. "Now take it out of my pants and ride it."

"With pleasure," I purr as I unzip his pants. Once they're undone, I push them and his boxer briefs down past his knees, then take his shaft into my hand, stroking it in a tight fist a few times.

"Damn that feels so good," Sax grunts before his fingers get to work unzipping my sleeveless leather dress all the way down the center until it's completely open and falls to the floor, leaving me in nothing but my panties.

All it takes is Sax's finger hooking in the side of the lacy crotch to pull them to the side and then he watches my face, waiting for me to lower myself down on him. I take him inside of me slowly, savoring every inch, knowing this will be the last time we'll be together like this.

My eyes slam shut as my body stretches and he fills me up so deeply I can barely breath.

Finally, when I'm fully seated on him, I blink open my eyes to look at Sax's face as I start to ride him. Just before I start to move, something outside of the bars catches my eye. There's a young, uniformed sheriff's deputy standing in the hallway watching us.

Leaning my lips forward to Sax's ear, I whisper, "We have an observer."

"Oh yeah?" he asks, not sounding all that surprised since we're in a cell with only prison bars separating us from the rest of the room. "Want me to run him off?" he asks while both of his hands come up to cup my bare breasts and give them a squeeze, making me gasp and my inner walls tighten around his still fully sheathed cock.

"No," I reply. "Having someone watch is making this even hotter."

"Then let's give him a good fucking show," Sax says, releasing one of my breasts to give my ass cheek a loud, burning slap. "Fuck me until you come so hard and loud, he makes a hot little mess in his pants."

"Yes, sir," I agree as I grip Sax's firm shoulders for support. I lift my hips until his cock almost slips out of me before slamming back down on him again so hard that I cry out.

"More. Fuck yes," Sax growls through gritted teeth as I slide up and down his cock faster and faster.

Neither of us are capable of words after that, only grunts and groans as we race toward the finish line because we feel so fucking good together. Sax watches my face with heavy-lidded eyes as his hands roam urgently over my breasts, down my sides and around to my ass like he can't decide what part of me he enjoys more.

Every once in a while, I sneak a peek over at our voyeur and nearly come when I watch him undo his brown uniform pants to shove his hand down inside. He's so turned on watching us that he was forced to give himself some relief. God, there's something incredibly hot about watching an attractive guy, a law-abiding sheriff's deputy, jacking off while Sax is buried inside of me. Just watching us is making him so horny he can't help himself. If all three of us get off, does this count as a ménage à trois? It's close enough that I plan to check it off my bucket list later.

"Both of us are about to make you come, aren't we?" Sax asks as he glances over his shoulder at the guard and then back to me. He doesn't sound jealous. No, it's more like he's intrigued and also titillated by the notion.

"Yes," I answer.

"God, you're perfect," Sax says before his mouth leans forward and his teeth close around my nipple, making me let loose a scream just as my pussy starts to clench around his thick cock. He sucks on my breast through my entire orgasm, dragging it out longer than any before.

Then, when my body goes limp against his, Sax grips my hips tightly and thrusts his shaft upward as deep as he can go. While he growls my name, I feel the warm pulses of his release filling me, so hot and thick I almost come again. But this is it, I've already enjoyed the last orgasm this man can give me. Three times with Sax may have been too many, because it's nearly impossible for me to release the hold I have on his shoulders.

Hearing a choked grunting noise, I glance over and watch as the guard plants his free hand on the wall and then shoots his cum onto the paint.

"He's making a mess...on the wall," I whisper to Sax.

"Good for him," he says with a chuckle before his palms cup both of my ass cheeks, squeezing them hard while his mouth finds mine for a hot, sensual kiss.

When he finally pulls away a few minutes later, Sax says, "If being watched wasn't on your bucket list, it should've been."

"No shit," I agree with a smile that he kisses swiftly.

"Now what are we going to do for the remaining seven hours I told Jade to keep us in here?" he asks.

"We should probably clean up," I suggest. "And then we can cuddle in the tiny, rock-like bed to soak up all the happiness we can from those hard-earned endorphins."

"Deal," Sax agrees with a goofy grin that's adorable and worrisome. It can only be sex between us, nothing else.

But I get the feeling that this man is different, and I may never forget him when I leave tomorrow.

CHAPTER ELEVEN

Sax

I'm not all that concerned when Gabe doesn't answer his cell or shop phone the first time I try him. It's early, before he's supposed to open up, so he's probably out.

I start to worry half an hour later when he's still not picking up.

"What's wrong?" Isobel asks when she comes up on the boat's deck wearing nothing but one of my t-shirts after our joint-shower following our short stint in jail. Imagining her leaving me later today and never coming back is unbearable, not just because everyone I care about will end up spending the rest of their lives in prison, but because I'm truly starting to care about her.

"Gabe isn't answering his phone, which is unusual," I tell Isobel when I wrap my arm around her waist to pull her onto my lap.

"Why is that unusual? Don't most people text nowadays?" she jokes with a smile.

"Maybe, but the Savage Kings have burner phones that only we use, pretty much for emergencies or whatever. And he's not answering in the shop where he also lives."

"I'm sure you'll get him soon."

"Yeah," I agree. "Let's just head on over," I suggest since my gut says that something *is* wrong. If we get to the shop and Gabriel isn't there or hasn't called me back, I'll try to get in touch with his brother Abe to see if he knows where he's gone.

"THIS IS THE PLACE?" Isobel asks when we pull up to Savage Ink's empty parking lot and I kill my bike's engine.

"It is, but Gabe's bike's not here. He must still be out," I tell her. "The shop officially opens in five minutes, so he should be back any minute."

I'm off my bike first, holding out my palm to help Isobel down. Her hand is still in mine when I feel a few of her fingers twitch.

"You okay?" I ask her in concern.

"Yeah, yeah," she replies quickly, pulling her hand away from mine to tug on the hem of her dress. "I'm just a little nervous about the needle I guess."

"There's nothing to it," I assure her. "Although your hip may be a little more sensitive than my back." When she remains quiet, her eyes downcast, staring at the pavement, lost in her own thoughts, I ask, "Are you still sure you want to do this? You don't have to."

"No, I'm ready," she says, lifting her face to mine with a smile now curving her lips. "I was just thinking that I'll be glad to get back to my car afterward so I can change clothes."

"I personally love the leather dress," I tell her, winding my arm around her waist to drag her body up against mine.

"I sort of prefer jeans and a tee," Isobel says.

"Bet you're sexy as hell in those too." I've just pressed my lips to the side of her neck when the sound of a revving engine interrupts. "That's probably Gabe," I tell her before his Harley is even in sight.

A second later, he whips it into the parking lot, in a hurry since he's almost late to open. Spotting us, he lifts one hand to wave.

"How embarrassing," Isobel leans up to whisper in my ear as Gabe parks next to my bike. "You two are wearing the *exact* same outfit."

Smiling, I jokingly say to her, "Then I guess I'll just have to insist that he change into something else."

"Hey, man, I didn't know you were waiting for me," Gabe tells us as he climbs off his bike and quickly removes his helmet. Tucking it under his arm, he retrieves his flip phone from the inside zipper of his cut. "Missed your calls while I was on the road too," he says, holding up the device with the notifications on the screen.

"Sorry to drop in like this with no notice, Gabe," I start. "But Isobel here was hoping you could maybe ink her today."

"Sure thing," he says as his dark eyes swing over to the girl in my arms. "I've got an hour or so free this morning. How big of a piece are we talking?" he asks, putting his phone away to pull his keys out of his jean pocket as the three of us start walking toward the front door.

Neither Isobel nor I get a chance to answer before the earth-shaking *BOOM* erupts behind us.

"Oh fuck," Gabriel mutters as we all spin around at the sound and see the black smoke billowing into the air about half a mile down the strip. "Was that..." he starts. "Do you think that was Avalon?"

"God, I hope not," I mutter. "Let's go find out," I say, wrapping my arm around Isobel's shoulders and guiding her to the motorcycle just as an invisible force from behind us knocks us to the ground. It only takes me a few seconds to realize the cause of it and then I'm diving on top of Isobel, covering her as a roaring blast of heat passes over us and unknown objects rain down on my back and my head. I'm guessing it's shards of glass from the windows along with pieces of bricks that were once the walls of Gabe's tattoo studio.

"Sax?" Isobel shouts fearfully from underneath me.

"Are you okay?" I ask her.

"Y-yeah, I-I think so," she stammers, her voice shaking. At least, I think that's what she says. My ears are filled with a high-pitched keening, that thankfully begins to fade after a few moments.

"Just stay still a little longer. I'm gonna get us out of here soon," I promise her.

Once the worst of the debris seems to have fallen down on us, I lift my head to glance over and check on Gabe.

He's lying face down on the ground, arms covering the back of his head to protect it while shouting a string of profanities.

"You still in one piece?" I ask him.

"Yeah, you?" he replies as he lowers his hands to the pavement to push himself up into a sitting position.

"I think so," I respond, lifting my weight off of Isobel so she can breathe.

"Sorry if I hurt you," I tell her when I get to my feet and offer Isobel a hand up. "Are you all right?"

"No. No, I'm fine," she says while dusting tiny pieces of gravel from her knees that are raw and scraped.

"What the fuck just happened?" Gabe exclaims as he puts his phone to his ear. "Shit," he mutters. "Coop's not answering!"

"I'll try Torin," I say since the clubhouse is right across the street from Avalon. If he's there, he'll be the closest who can help. "You need to call Abe right now and let him know you're safe before he hears about the studio from someone else and panics," I tell Gabriel.

"Yeah, okay," he murmurs. "Dammit, now I can't remember his number. Oh, right."

I try to remove my own phone from my cut, but fuck if my hands aren't still shaking with adrenaline. I know without a doubt that if Gabe hadn't been running late, the three of us would have been inside, and all of us would be seriously fucked up, if not dead. Isobel could've died, and it would've been my fault for bringing her here.

"Are you sure you're okay?" I ask her as she stands frozen, staring at the flames shooting out of the shop.

"This...this is why you need a bucket list," she says, her eyes wide and face stunned. "We almost...we could've..."

"God, I'm so damn sorry this happened," I tell her as I wind my left arm around her, clutching my phone in my right hand while I hold her to me.

"Why? Who would do something like this?" she lifts her face to mine and asks, her greenish-blue eyes sad, scared and confused.

And just like that, a name comes to mind.

Her father's not so fucking insane that he would come after the Savage King businesses I just told him about last night, is he?

I need to find out if Avalon was hit too; because if so, the other Kings' buildings could be at risk.

"What?" Isobel asks. "What was that look? You know who did this?"

"No," I reply since I'm not one hundred percent sure yet. "I'm just worried about the other Kings." Keeping one arm around her, I flip open my phone and try to call Torin, and then his brother, Chase, our VP, when he doesn't answer. Both of the calls go straight to voicemail.

"I can't believe it," Gabe whispers across from us, pacing with the phone to his ear as he watches what's left of his tattoo shop burn to the ground. "I can't fucking believe it! Everything I own just *POOF*, gone," he grumbles before his brother must pick up. "Abe, holy shit bro, you won't believe what just happened! I'm okay, but my shop sure as hell is not. It just blew up! Had to be a bomb or some shit in a planned attack because we think Avalon may have been hit too."

My next phone call is to Reece, our all-knowing IT expert.

"Can't really talk right now, Sax," Reece says when he thankfully answers the phone after several rings. "Avalon just went up in fucking flames!"

"Is everyone whole? Cooper okay? Was he in there?" I ask him in a rush.

"Coop is pretty fucked up," he says. "Torin and Cedric just pulled him out of the rubble and loaded him into the van," he says. "Torin doesn't want to take him to the hospital until we find out who the hell did this, so we're taking him to the safehouse in Sandy

Creek. He needs a doctor bad. He's rambling and shit, in a lot of pain. There's a ton of shrapnel in his arms and chest that we're gonna have to dig out."

"Shit," I mutter, understanding Torin's concern even though it sucks. We can't protect Cooper if he's out in public where anyone can ask and find his room to finish the job. But he needs some type of medical attention. Isobel's hand rubs soothing circles over the back of my cut, like she knows I need the comfort. Which is when it hits me that she could help Coop. It's perfect, actually. Almost too perfect...

Without another thought, I tell Reece, "I'm with a nurse right now over at Gabe's. His shop blew up too, but we were all standing outside when it happened. We'll meet you at the safehouse in half an hour."

"You're with a nurse? Fuck, that's lucky. See ya then, man," Reece says when he ends the call.

As soon as Isobel's hand freezes and then she takes a step back out of my arms, I know I've fucked up.

"How...how did you know I'm a nurse?" she asks softly, eyes wide in surprise.

"You're not the only one who takes precautions with lovers," I hedge. "I looked you up on the internet, saw that photo of you with a bunch of kids in Africa or whatever getting vaccines."

"Oh," she mutters, her voice telling me she's still not convinced.

"It wasn't hard to figure out your last name since you're the governor's daughter," I point out. "You are a nurse, right?" I ask, finally letting myself look at her face.

"Yeah, I am. I was," she answers quickly with a shake of her head.

"Why did you give it up?"

"Long story," Isobel says with a wave of her hand. "Why don't you tell me what's happened and where we're going?"

"One of our brothers, Cooper, manages Avalon, a strip club the Savage Kings MC owns right down the road where that first explosion was. He was inside the club when this shit happened," I say, waving a hand toward the smoke in the distance.

"How badly is he injured? Why aren't they taking him to the hospital?" she asks.

"Shrapnel is all Reece said; and until we know who attacked us, it's not safe for any of us to be in public. That could just make a hospital a target."

"I'm a pediatric nurse. What if I can't help him?" she asks.

"If you think he needs to go to the hospital, then we'll take him to one out of state, or whatever we need to do," I tell her. "Okay?"

"Okay," she agrees.

"Gabe!" I yell to get his attention since he's still on the phone, probably with his brother asking a million questions. "We need to get to the safehouse in Sandy Creek off of highway seventy-four," I say while Isobel and I get our helmets on. "Tell Abe to meet us there too."

Once he gives a nod, we hurry onto my bike and take off.

As PROMISED, I have us rolling up at the safehouse in less than thirty minutes. I pull down the driveway and ride around to the back of the house to park my bike with the row of other Harleys hidden from view.

"You were taking it easy on me before," Isobel says when she climbs off the back of the bike and stumbles. I jump off quickly and grab her arm to steady her.

"We weren't in a hurry before," I reply, removing her helmet and setting it on the seat to take her hand. "Come on," I tell her, leading her to the back door.

It opens before we get there. Then Torin is filling it, his pistol already in his hand.

"Who the fuck is she?" our president asks with a nod towards Isobel. Reece must not have filled him in. He even puts his free hand up on the door frame to keep us out.

"I'm the fucking nurse," Isobel responds before I can even open my mouth. She lets go of my hand and ducks down, slipping right underneath Torin's arm.

His jaw gapes as he turns and watches her disappear into the house. Not many people would ever think about standing up to our president. Straightening, Torin faces me again as he holsters his pistol. Crossing his arms over his chest, his green eyes narrow and his cheek ticks in annoyance before he says, "Explain who the hell that was."

"Her name is Isobel. I met her a few days ago, and she's a pediatric nurse. Or at least she used to be, but she's on a hiatus."

"She doesn't look like any nurse I've ever seen," he mutters.

"I think that's pretty much her goal," I tell him, remembering her comment about her current look being a costume. "But if she can help Cooper..."

"Yeah," he replies with a sigh, dropping his arms back to his sides. "Sorry. I'm just on edge since we don't have a goddamn clue who the fuck blew up Avalon."

"I know, I get it," I tell him. "Did Reece tell you about Gabe's shop?"

"What about Gabe's shop?" Torin asks.

"Savage Ink blew up while Isobel, Gabe and I were standing outside of it. We weren't hurt, but the shop is toast."

"Goddamn it!" he exclaims before spinning around to slam his fist into the siding.

"It's fucked up; but if anyone can figure it out, Reece can," I assure him.

"I had hoped Avalon went up because of a gas line or some shit. Guess that was naïve of me," Torin grumbles while cradling his now bloody knuckles.

"How's Coop doing?" I ask.

"He was lucky," Torin replies. "From across the street, we didn't think it was possible for anyone to survive and hoped he hadn't come in to work yet. But then we saw his bike, and there he was under a pile of debris on the backside of what was left of the building."

"Fuck," I grumble as I swipe the sweat from my brow.

"Peyton told Dalton that the ATF is all over this shit already, wanting us to answer questions, tell them who could've been behind it."

Sighing as I inwardly cringe when I think of who may be to blame, I say, "And we can't exactly sit down and turn over a list of our enemies without implicating ourselves in a fuck ton of crimes."

"Exactly," Torin replies. "Most of the guys are inside. The women and kids are heading back to the safehouse in South Carolina, which I absolutely fucking hate because we can't protect them there. But Cooper was in too much pain to make it down to South Carolina. And there's just not enough room here. Besides, we can't take the chance of any of us leading whoever is behind this disaster home."

"Right, yeah," I agree after he finishes his rant. "Shit!" I yell when I suddenly remember I haven't done my job. "I need to get a message out to the other charters."

"You haven't done that yet?" he asks incredulously. "Good thing the women all had each other's phone numbers!"

"Sorry. I'll do it right this second," I tell him as I rush to get my phone in my hands, praying that there haven't been any attacks in any other cities with Savage Kings charters. "What should we say?" I ask. "Just tell them that Avalon was blown up and to increase security on all Savage Kings establishments until further notice?"

"That's all we *can* say right now," he agrees with a nod. "You should ask them to report any other attacks in their area, and maybe mention that one brother was injured, but should make a full recovery so they won't panic, thinking we've been wiped out."

"Okay," I say as I quickly type it all into an email and then send it to the entire Savage King list, which goes to around two thousand members nationwide. "There. Done."

CHAPTER TWELVE

Isobel

I don't have to ask where the injured Savage King is. The crowd gathered in the hallway at the first bedroom is the dead giveaway.

"Excuse me," I say to the dark-haired man covered in tats. "Coming through."

"Sorry," he grunts when he turns around and we're face to face. Frowning down at me, he says, "Hold up. Who the hell are you?"

"Jeez, are you all this polite?" I mutter. "I'm with Sax and I'm a nurse, so do you want me to see if I can help your friend or not?"

"Sorry," he mutters again. Not only does he step aside, he also shouts, "Get your asses out of the way! Nurse coming through!"

The rest of the guys in leather vests listen to him, making a path for me to squeeze into the room where a shirtless man in torn jeans is laying on the center of a queen-sized bed. He's bleeding from the cuts and slashes on his face, arms and torso. When I'm by his side, his glazed over, pale blue eyes meet mine. "J-jenna?" he croaks softly.

"Ah, no. I'm Isobel and I'm a nurse. Can you tell where it hurts the most," I say slowly and clearly before I lift his wrist to take his pulse. Only once the words leave my mouth do I realize I'm talking to him like a child.

"No!" he exclaims, jerking his hand out of my grip. "Jenna! Help Jenna first!"

I turn to look at the faces of the men standing around us to see if Jenna is here, and if I need to check on her first. One of the guys with a reddish-blond beard and sad green eyes gives a slight shake of his head. So either they didn't find her yet or he's delusional.

Well, that really sucks. And I don't want to upset the guy even more.

Grabbing his hand again, I tell him, "Jenna's worried about you," I lie. "Let me see how you're doing so I can let her know."

His confused eyes watch my lips and then he shouts, "What? What's going on? I can't hear you! Where's Jenna?"

"He's been like this since we found him," the red bearded guy speaks up and says. "We keep telling him what happened, over and over again, and he keeps asking us and wanting to know about someone named Jenna."

"Does anyone have a flashlight?" I ask when I realize what could be the problem. Then, I remember my phone is in my purse hanging across the front of my body and quickly pull it out. Turning on the light app, I hold it up to the injured man's right ear and then lean over him to look at the left one. "His ears are bleeding," I tell his friends. "I think his eardrums may have blown, which explains why he's shouting and not able to understand what we're telling him. He can't hear us."

"Fuck," a buff guy with a shaved head who looks ex-military says. "Is it permanent?"

"I can't say for sure. Sometimes after a trauma there's improvement within a few days and some, if not all, hearing returns to normal. Sometimes there can be a significant loss, though. We'll just have to wait and see."

"What supplies do you need?" the military man asks me.

"An antiseptic solution to start cleaning out the cuts would be good. Gauze and bandages to cover them, a thermometer, and ah, an intravenous sedative or pain reliever if you have it?"

"I'll see what Eddie has and have him get his ass over here," the man tells me before he slips out and makes room for Sax to come in.

"Jesus," Sax mutters when he sees his buddy. "Anyone see who did this?"

"Not yet," Red Beard replies. "Reece said it's a fucking ghost, for all we know. Just a man in a black hoodie that went into the club last night but never shows the cameras his face. No vehicle, so no plates either."

"Oh shit," Gabe, the tattoo artist mutters when he joins us in the bedroom. "A guy in a black hoodie wearing a backpack came in the shop last night," he tells the group. "He asked to use the bathroom, and I was in the middle of a back tat, so I just told him to have at it. I didn't even get a good look at him."

"Goddamn it," someone groans.

"He must have put a bomb up in the air vents or some shit," another person opines.

"So far we haven't heard from any other charters about similar attacks," Sax tells the room when everyone goes quiet. "So at least there's that."

"Which means it's personal," the big, angry guy from the back door says when he comes into the room. Everyone's attention turns to him, like he's the one in charge, a man they look up to. "Someone's coming after *our* charter, and we need to figure out who they are and how to stop them. Right now Jade has sheriff's deputies stationed outside of the clubhouse, hotel and salvage yard. But there aren't enough uniforms to watch all of our homes. All we can do is hope that's all the destruction they planned for us." Facing me, he says, "Thanks for taking care of Cooper. I really hope we can trust you."

"You can," Sax says before I can even reassure him. And even with everything going on, I can tell that there's something he isn't telling us. Sax has an idea who did this but wouldn't tell me.

And I would have to be an idiot not to have a pretty good guess who it is myself.

Would my father risk *killing* people just because he doesn't like the man I lied and told him I'm in love with?

Now I wish I had never asked Sax to go along with such a stupid idea with the sole intention of pissing off my father because it may have seriously backfired.

CHAPTER THIRTEEN

Sax

"The nurse is a keeper," War says when we all head to the backyard to wait for Abe, our last member to arrive, so we can talk shit over as a group.

"You think so?" I ask, even though I already know Isobel is. My problem isn't wanting to keep her but convincing her to stop running.

"Yeah, she looks like a woman who can roll with the punches. And it would be nice to have a nurse around twenty-four-seven."

"No shit," I snort. "But Isobel is a free-spirit. I'm not sure if she's the type to settle down."

Slapping his hand on my shoulder, he says, "Man, if Dalton can do it, anyone can."

"Maybe so," I agree since our brother was the biggest player on the planet until he met Peyton.

The roar of his motorcycle barely proceeds Abe as he whips into the backyard, having obviously sped all the way here. He's off his bike a second later, throwing his arms around his brother before he even removes his helmet.

It was a close call, so I know he's glad the kid wasn't hurt.

"Who the fuck did this?" Abe roars when he releases Gabe. "Who the fuck tried to hurt my little brother? I'll rip their fucking head off with my bare hands!"

"Chill, man. We don't know yet," Chase says when he goes over to calm his best friend down.

"Gather around!" Torin says. "This is a conversation that doesn't need to be overheard."

We all come together in a tight circle, like a football team huddling up. "I think it's pretty obvious that we're all thinking the same thing about who could be behind this shit today."

"Russians," Miles grumbles, causing me to release a pent-up sigh of relief.

The fucking Russians! Why didn't I think of them? They have more motive to hurt us than an angry governor.

"We knew retaliation was a possibility since we couldn't take all of them out without flying to the other side of the world," Torin responds. "But honestly, I thought they would have to be insane to come after us with an attack of this magnitude. They're trying to cripple us, hit us in our pockets."

"I'll kill every one of those Russian mobsters!" Abe declares. "How's Cooper doing?"

"He seems stable enough to keep here. With Sax's nurse, it's safer than all of us crowding into a hospital," Torin declares.

"Until we know *exactly* who did this, we can't even go after them," Reece says. "If it is the leftover Russians, they're being careful, sending the one man in a hoodie to do the dirty work, which means our hands are fucking tied."

"Goddammit," Abe grumbles.

"I've talked to Ivan and he said he hasn't had any problems, so it looks like we're the sole focus, at least for now," Torin informs us. "Hopefully we can get a handle on things and take them down before they do any more damage. Until we know more, no one leaves here alone."

"What about the women?" Miles asks.

"Every Savage King in Myrtle Beach is going to be guarding them. We could bring in additional guys from Wilmington; but the more men we put on them, the more attention we draw."

"MB has what, ten members?" Chase asks.

"Twelve patched and four prospects," I tell him since I keep up with the stats on all charters.

"If sixteen armed men can't keep our people safe, then we're all fucked anyway," Chase replies.

"Why can't we be the ones down there protecting them?" Miles asks.

"Sure, Miles," War says. "Why don't we all drive right on down to the safehouse with a bullseye on each of our backs and lead these fuckers right to our old ladies and kids."

"I don't like Kira being away from me, especially when her belly's getting bigger every day," Miles huffs.

"Kira will be fine. The ladies will look after her, and she still has months to go, man," Chase says. "None of us like having our women in another state, but we can't be too careful." Turning to me, he then asks, "How much do you trust this nurse of yours?"

"She's the one in danger here since she was almost blown up at Gabe's," I point out defensively. "But since it's only a matter of time before Reece does his digging and you find out anyway, Isobel has ties to the governor."

Everyone goes silent, even the crickets.

"The currently elected North Carolina governor?" Maddox asks.

"Yes."

"How close of ties are we talking?" Reece whispers.

"Ah, well, he's her father," I respond.

"Motherfucker."

"Son of a bitch."

"Are you fucking serious?"

Various curses come from the mouths of every brother. "They're not close. Far from it," I assure them. "They're basically estranged. We can trust her."

When they continue to bitch and moan, I say, "Hey! At least she's not a federal agent, a news reporter, or a fucking social worker!"

Dalton, Chase and War all glare daggers at me for calling out their significant others.

"Fuck," Torin says as he scrubs his hands over his face. "You guys sure do know how to pick them."

"Says the man who married the daughter of our *enemy*," I throw back at him. "Look, we can trust Isobel, and it'll be good to have her around to keep an eye on Cooper; right?"

Yes, that's perfect actually. I can ask her to stick around to watch over Cooper until he recovers. It'll be a great excuse for her to stay with me, and it's in our boy's best interest too.

"Fine," Torin grits out. "But you have to take her phone from her and make sure she never speaks a word to *anyone* about what she sees or hears while she's with us."

"That shouldn't be a problem," I tell him just as Eddie pulls up in his tow truck, hopefully with the supplies Isobel asked for.

Isobel

"How's HE DOING?" Sax asks after I've finished cleaning and bandaging the last cut and am pulling the sheets over Cooper.

"He's finally resting," I tell him, thanks to the pain meds Eddie, the older gentleman, brought me. "None of the wounds are very deep, but they're ugly and inflamed, so there's still a risk of infection." Standing up, I remove my latex gloves, then toss them into the trash can one of the guys brought into the room. Turning to Sax, I brace my hands on my hips to give him a rundown on future care. "Someone will need to change the dressing on all twelve of the lacerations and apply more antibiotic ointment to them twice a day, as well as monitor his temperature every few hours for a fever. Then, once he improves enough to travel, he'll need to see a specialist about his loss of hearing."

"I know just the person for the job," Sax says with a grin. "She's amazing and beautiful with a medical background."

"Well, ah, good," I say with only a hint of jealousy for the woman he thinks is amazing and beautiful. What do I care when I'm leaving today? "I can talk to her before I leave if you want."

"I was referring to you, Isobel," he replies, slipping his hands in the front of his jeans and looking too good to be true, sexy with just enough of the bad boy image thanks to the leather.

"Sorry, Sax, but you know I can't stay." I have to decline, despite how good he looks.

"Can't you postpone your journey for just a few days?" he asks, giving me big, blue puppy dog eyes. "Please?"

"He's going to be fine," I assure him, glancing over at his sleeping friend.

"I'd feel so much better if you were here to make sure," Sax says. "So would the other guys. And as soon as Gabe replaces his tattoo gun and supplies, he could give you that cherry blossom and butterfly you wanted, right here in the house."

"I can't, Sax," I say on a sigh. "I'm scheduled to sing at a bar in Charlotte tomorrow, then catch a flight to the UK for the International Balloon Fiesta."

"You can't or won't stay?" Sax asks. "I'm sure you could reschedule with the bar."

"I don't like going back on my word when I agree to do something," I tell him.

"It's not going back on your word, just postponing for a few days," he says. "And I bet you haven't even booked a flight for the UK yet, have you?"

"The event is only a week away, and I can't miss it. Today was scary and reminded me just how short life is," I declare, refusing to budge.

"So then you can stay for, what, five days and still make the flight in time?" Sax asks. "Sometimes being spontaneous is about breaking rules, right? Even your own."

Sitting down slowly on the edge of the bed to avoid jostling Cooper, I sigh as I stare up at the sexiest man I've ever met. I need to move on, to put miles between me and Sax before I grow even more attached to him. But for whatever reason, I find myself caving. "My car has probably been towed by the bar by now. I need to get it so I can finally change my clothes."

"Done," Sax says, his face lighting up with equal parts relief and joy. Holding out his hand, palm up, he says, "Give me your keys, and I'll go get it right now."

"Right now?" I repeat.

"Yes. You can stay here to keep an eye on Cooper, and I'll get the prospect to give me a ride down in the van."

"Okay," I say as I go grab my purse I hung on the closet door and pull out the keyring. "Thanks," I tell Sax when I drop them in his outstretched hand.

"No, beautiful. Thank you for agreeing to stay," he says before he turns to leave.

"Only for five days," I remind him. "Less, if he's up and around before then."

"I know," Sax says when he pauses to look at me over his shoulder. "No matter how long you're here for, I'm going to enjoy every fucking second."

He then turns and walks out of the room. Just the sound of the back door opening and closing makes my chest tight. I miss him already, and he hasn't even left the property yet.

This is bad.

I've got it bad for Sax, and I just agreed to spend more time with him.

"What the hell is wrong with me?" I ask aloud to myself before I slump down on the foot of the bed again. "You need to get better fast, buddy," I tell the sleeping man.

The truth is, if I left and something happened to Cooper, I would feel awful and blame myself for leaving him unattended. These stubborn men should have taken him to the hospital, but I understand their reluctance after being only a few feet away from one explosion. They're jumpy, worried what else may be coming at them, with no idea who it is that's hurting them.

And maybe part of me is staying close to the Savage Kings until they rule out my father's involvement. I could never forgive myself if he's the one responsible for nearly killing one of Sax's friends.

ABOUT HALF AN HOUR after Sax leaves, I'm placing my hand on Cooper's forehead and chest again to check for warmth indicating a fever when I hear a man's raised voice from the living room. The rest of the guys cleared out of the bedroom so that Cooper could rest, but they obviously didn't go far.

"There's some attorney at the clubhouse asking where Cooper is. Jade said she's pretty worked up and is refusing to leave until she gets an answer," a deep voice says to the others.

"Is she short and stacked? Blonde? Liz something or another?" another voice asks, and the first guy repeats that information back like he's on the phone talking to someone.

"Yeah, she is. You know her?"

Curious, and bored since Cooper is still out cold, I slip down the hallway to listen in on their conversation.

"Yeah," the guy with tattoos on his arms, head and neck says. "She's cool. Her and Cooper are fuck buddies."

"Any objections to giving her this address?" Red Beard asks the guys in the room with the phone up to his ear.

"Yes," the grumpy man in charge who originally tried to keep me out of the house says. "Someone could follow her from the clubhouse to here."

"If she's a lawyer, then I think she's smart enough to notice if she's being followed or not," Tattoo guy says. "And it might do Coop some good if she's here, having a friendly face and all."

"What's her name again?" the guy on the phone asks. "Elizabeth Townsend? Then why the fuck does Coop keep asking about a Jenna?"

"Is she one of the new dancers?" the grumpy man asks.

"Oh fuck. Jade, did the firefighters find anyone else in the building?" the man on the phone questions. "It was too early for any of the dancers to be there, right?"

When his face goes pale around his reddish facial hair, it's safe to guess he just got bad news.

"Jenna Higgins was found dead at Avalon," he informs the group. "The medical examiner told Jade she had a broken neck and spine, and likely died instantly when a beam from the ceiling fell on her. That must be why Coop keeps asking for her."

"Oh no," I gasp as I cover my mouth. Only after all the men turn to look at me do I realize that I must have said that out loud. "Sorry."

Ignoring me, the guy on the phone says, "So what's it going to be, Torin?"

"Tell the attorney to park two streets over on the corner of Sea Trail Road and Bishop. I'll meet her there on foot and walk her over here," Torin, I now know is his name, says.

"Jesus, Cooper," the blonde in a black pantsuit says when she freezes at the bedroom doorway. A second later, she's by his side, brushing his wavy, chin-length hair back from his face, her eyes scanning over all of the various bandages. "Is he...is he in a lot of pain?" she asks me.

"I don't think so. He's just sleeping. I gave him some morphine to take the edge off and make him more comfortable so he could rest."

"So he's going to be okay?" she asks.

"Yeah, I believe so. Most of the cuts are superficial. The biggest concern is his hearing."

"His hearing?" she repeats, her face crumbling even more.

"It looks like both of his eardrums were ruptured in the explosion. He couldn't seem to hear what we were saying to him and kept asking the same questions over and over."

"Oh no," she says as she sinks down to her knees next to the bed and clasps his hand in both of hers.

"The hearing loss could be temporary," I tell her, and she nods silently. Her face is hidden by the curtain of her sleek, shoulder-length blonde hair, but I don't have to see it to know that she's crying.

"I'll leave and give you some time alone," I say, suddenly feeling like an intruder.

Since the house is pretty full, I grab my phone from my purse and slip out the back door to take a seat on the deck steps, eagerly waiting for Sax to return. Before I forget, I send a text to the bar owner in Charlotte to postpone, apologizing profusely.

I still can't believe I agreed to stay for Sax, or that I'm glad to have a reason to hang around longer. For the first time since I started on this bucket list journey of mine, I was dreading leaving.

The door behind me eventually opens, and then the lawyer is coming out and slumping down on the step next to me. I think one of the guys said her name is Liz.

She doesn't say a word, so I wait patiently until she's ready to talk, if she decides to. Her occasional sniffles are heartbreaking.

"Do they know who did this?" she whispers.

"Not yet, I don't think."

"I hope they make them pay when they figure it out," she murmurs. The mention of retaliation coming from such an elegant looking business woman is somewhat shocking. "Wow, I can't believe I said that," Liz immediately adds, slapping her palm over her mouth.

"You must think I'm a horrible person. I guess I've just been sleeping with an outlaw for so long he's rubbing off on me in all sorts of ways."

"I'm sorry he was hurt," I tell her.

"Me too, he's a good man," she agrees with a sigh. "And I wish I knew who Jenna was. After you left the room, Cooper sort of, um, moaned her name."

"I overheard the guys say that she was one of the dancers at Avalon," I inform her.

"Oh." After several seconds she asks, "Do you think...I mean, it seems obvious that he was probably sleeping with her, right?"

"That I have no clue," I say. "All I know is that she was in the building when it exploded. And she didn't make it out."

"Oh god," Liz says on a gasp. "Now I feel like such a bitch for automatically disliking her."

"So you and Cooper are...seeing each other?" I ask.

"Only casually, you know? Nothing serious. How can you be serious with a man who manages a strip club and is around perfect, naked women all day?" she asks. "And I mean, why else would Jenna have been at the club *alone* with Cooper before noon when they don't even open until four?"

"Ah, no clue," I say honestly. "Just because one possibility is that he was sleeping with her doesn't mean he was. There are plenty of other reasons why she was with him."

"Like what?" she asks.

"Um, well, maybe she was practicing her routine."

The side-eye look Liz gives me is highly skeptical.

"Could it have been payday?" I ask. "Or maybe she left her phone there the night before and went to pick it up. Who knows? Don't drive yourself crazy thinking the worst until you know for sure."

"Thanks for talking me off the cliff," Liz says with a pat to my forearm. "The messed up thing is that it doesn't even matter if Cooper was sleeping with her or all of the girls. He could've died today, and I can't imagine never seeing him again."

"He's going to have a tough recovery ahead of him, especially when he realizes his hearing has been compromised for however long and he finds out about Jenna," I tell her. "I'm sure he would appreciate having you around to help him through it."

"Thanks," she says with a heavy sigh. "I just realized I don't even know your name. I'm Elizabeth, by the way," she says, offering me her palm that I take.

"I'm Isobel, Sax's friend," I reply. "And in another lifetime, I was a nurse. That's what brought me here."

"The Savage Kings didn't want Cooper in a hospital where cops would want to ask him questions," she says with a nod of understanding.

"That and they're all vulnerable until they catch the person responsible. If someone wanted them all dead, it wouldn't be hard to hit the hospital. I don't think they're just looking out for themselves."

"Yeah," Liz agrees. "That makes sense in a horrible way I guess."

CHAPTER FOURTEEN

Sax

As soon as I'm alone in Isobel's Lexus, which was thankfully still parked at the bar in Myrtle Beach, I call the number her father texted the address from.

"This better be important," Governor Washington snaps when he answers.

"Your daughter nearly died today, so yeah, I would consider it important," I tell him. He's silent, and I can't tell if that's because he doesn't know about the explosions or if he's kicking himself in the ass for not considering that Isobel could be inside one of the buildings he blew up.

"What happened?" he eventually asks.

"Avalon and Savage Ink were blown all to hell today. Did you do it?" I ask him through gritted teeth.

"No," he answers. "Was Isobel hurt?"

"We were outside the tattoo studio when it happened, so no," I respond and hear his audible exhale of relief. So his heart isn't completely cold and shriveled up.

"Why would you think I'm responsible?" he asks. "I'm trying to get reelected, which is highly unlikely if I blow things up, even shitty biker bars. Were there any fatalities?"

"No. As far as I know, just one King was injured," I say since Avalon was still closed when it happened. Although, that could be why Coop kept asking about someone named Jenna.

"I'll look into it," he says. "If someone almost hurt my daughter, then I'll make sure they're caught and pay for their mistake."

Judging from his offer to look into it and from his tone, I believe he may actually be telling the truth. He may hate that Isobel and I are together, but he's the one that set it up. There's no good reason for why he would blow our businesses up. Guess the Russians are at the top of our list of suspects.

"Could it be Russian retaliation?" the governor asks, thinking the same thing.

"Possibly. We wiped out most of the important members of Kozlov's syndicate, although it's possible they could be regrouping."

"I'll see what I can find out and let you know," he says. "How are things going otherwise?" he asks. "Isobel is pretending you're her boyfriend and actually came home, so you must have made a good impression."

"Her nursing skills are coming in handy today. I'm doing the best I can, but she's pretty set on getting to the United Kingdom within a week's time."

"Then you better come up with a plan to stop her. I need her to start making a few appearances on the campaign trail and back me with her mother's trust fund."

"You told me my job was to get her to settle down and go back to nursing, not work for you and pay for your fucking campaign!" I shout at him through the phone.

"One and the same. If Isobel stays, there's no reason she can't support my reelection."

That's what he thinks. From what I can tell, she loathes her father and doesn't want anything to do with him or his campaign despite the fact that I was able to convince her to go see him on his birthday.

"You're a dick, you know that?" I ask him, but his only response is to laugh and hang up on me.

∼

Isobel

Liz and I are still hanging out on the steps, talking about everything and nothing when the black van pulls back up, followed by my car.

"Yay!" I stand up and cheer, not just because this means I can finally put on a pair of jeans, but I'm also happy to see Sax again when he shuts off the engine and opens the driver door. The delight is also accompanied by a jolt of desire, wanting to be with him, to feel his warm hard body on top of mine.

Which is stupid because he's already given me enough orgasms to make me start feeling an attachment to him. I blame that attachment for convincing me to sleep with Sax again tonight, even though it's a bad idea.

I'm getting ready to go down the steps to greet him and tell him my idiotic decision when the back door opens, and then my phone is suddenly plucked from my hand.

"What are you still doing with this?" Torin grumbles. "What is she still doing with this?" he shouts at Sax as he approaches us.

"Sorry, I forgot," Sax answers with a wince.

"Forgot what?" I ask as I stand up.

"We need to keep your phone while you're here."

"Why?" I ask.

"Because someone could be tracking you, or you could be sending photos and shit to our enemies," Torin huffs.

"Wow. Paranoid much?" I ask.

"Yours too," Torin says when he glances down at Liz.

"Don't worry, I'm leaving," she says when she gets to her feet. "Cooper needs to rest, so I'll take off."

"Are you sure?" I ask her since I know she's worried about him.

"Yeah, I just wanted to make sure he was still in one piece; but we're not together, and he may not even want me here when he wakes up."

"You could stop by tomorrow. Maybe he'll be more alert..." I suggest, but Torin instantly shoots my idea down.

"No," he says. "I don't want a bunch of people coming and going from here until we neutralize the threat."

"Understood," Liz says as she swipes at the dirt on the back of her suit pants. "Will you just let Cooper know I came by and that I hope he recovers soon?"

"Sure," I promise her before she jogs down the steps.

"Cedric, walk with her to her car over on Sea Trail Road," Torin orders before he turns around and stomps back into the house while Sax comes up to the porch.

"Sorry," he says when he takes my hand and pulls me down the steps and over to the picnic table in the backyard. "Torin's in charge, and he's a little on edge."

"No, I get it," I reply. "I'm new, and he doesn't trust me. He has enough to worry about with his injured friend and dead dancer."

Sax's blue eyes bulge. "What dead dancer?"

"Oh, ah, you haven't heard yet?" I say, remembering he was retrieving my car when we found out. "A woman named Jenna was in the building with Cooper when it exploded. Someone told the guys they thought she probably died instantly."

"Jesus," Sax mutters. "That's why Coop was asking about her. Wait, who was that woman sitting with you on the steps?"

"Liz. Her and Cooper have been seeing each other."

"Oh. I didn't know he was seeing anyone."

"Yeah, the other guys didn't know either, just the one with tattoos on his neck and head."

"Miles," Sax says. "That's Miles. I should probably introduce you to everyone since you're going to be around for a while."

"That would be nice," I tell him. "I do know Cooper, Gabe and Torin's name. Who is Red Beard?"

"Red Beard?" Sax repeats. "Oh, that's Chase, Torin's brother."

"Got it," I say. "Black beard?"

"Abe, Gabriel's brother."

"And the military-looking guys, one with black hair and one mostly shaved?" I ask.

"Mostly shaved is Reece, and darker hair is Warren or War."

"And the, um...preppy guy?"

Groaning, Sax huffs, "Go ahead and say what you meant. The *hot* guy? Isn't that what you wanted to say?"

"Fine," I agree. "The incredibly handsome blond man who looks like he could be your brother."

That makes Sax smile before he responds. "His name is Dalton," he says. "And you're so full of shit."

"So, that just leaves the two younger guys who haven't said much, one of which went with you in the van."

"The one with all the patches on his cut is Maddox, our newest member," Sax responds. "And the kid with the cut that only has the 'prospect' rocker on the lower back is Cedric."

"That's everyone, huh?" I say.

"All the brothers. Then there are the old ladies and kids..."

"Wow, I'll never remember all of their names," I admit.

"You'll learn," Sax says confidently as his arm winds around my waist to drag me up against the front of his body for a quick kiss on the lips. "Thank you for taking care of Cooper and agreeing to stay. I'm sorry for putting you in danger."

"The occasional danger makes you appreciate life even more," I reply. "And close calls like that make me want to seek comfort from sexy men in leather."

"What kind of comfort?" he asks with a grin.

"Oh, I think you know the kind," I answer coyly.

His tongue sneaks out to wet his lips and then he says, "What about your rule?"

"Turns out rules are just another type of prison. There's no reason to let anything hold me back from getting what I want. And I want...you."

That's apparently all the explanation Sax needed, because the next thing I know, he's lifting me off the ground and throwing me over his shoulder before he strides toward the house.

"You can get me naked," I tell his backside since I'm now hanging upside down. "But then I'm taking a shower and you're gonna have to bring my clothes in from my car!"

"Maybe I'll just hide your dress and keep you naked for a few days," he says when he opens the back door and takes us inside.

There's soft masculine laughter from the living room when we walk through. "God, I miss my wife," someone says with a heavy sigh.

"Just a warning, any screams you gentleman hear will be from passion. I'll try to keep it down, but no promises," I tell the guys as we make our way down the hallway.

"Like hell you will," Sax scoffs. "Challenge accepted!"

"Great. Thanks for the fucking reminder of all the sexless days ahead of us, Sax!" a voice calls back.

CHAPTER FIFTEEN

Sax

As soon as Isobel and I clear the bedroom, I shut the door and lower her feet back to the floor.

Whatever I was expecting to happen next, it wasn't having her grab either side of my cut and pulling me against her body to kiss the fuck out of me, but I can't say I'm opposed.

After our lips and tongues lock, a frenzy begins. Both of us try to rip the other's clothes off faster than the other. I win since all I have to do is slide the zipper down the center of her dress.

"I'm never wearing that dress again," Isobel declares when the leather hits the floor.

"That would be a shame," I tell her as she removes my cut and yanks my shirt up over my head.

Without giving her time to unzip my jeans, I drop to my knees in front of her and spear the tip of my tongue into the apex of her thighs, so damn glad she decided to toss her thong into the trash after the mess we made at the jail.

"Sax, oh my god," Isobel moans, the door thumping when her head falls back and hits it.

"Have you missed my tongue here?" I ask while slipping my index finger through her folds.

"Yes," she gasps as I ease the digit inside of her wet cunt. "More. Please," she begs, asking me to lower my mouth back down to her flesh. I tease her a little longer, adding another finger that I plunge in and out of her tight pussy.

"Oh, god, please!" she screams, her hips writhing, fucking my fingers. Since her moans are starting to sound desperate, I give her what she needs – a swipe of my tongue down her slit and back up again where I flick the tip over her swollen clit.

"Yes! Right there!" she shouts as her fingers spear through my hair and then tighten on the strands, holding my head right where she needs it so I'll keep licking her. Like I could ever get enough. The woman is wild and beautiful and so damn compassionate. Not to mention she has the sexiest body I've ever had the pleasure of seeing, touching, and tasting.

When Isobel's hips start bucking, I know she's getting close, so I increase the speed and force of my tongue until her gasps and pants turn into a scream and her legs quake. I lap up every drop of her arousal that she gives me before plunging my tongue deep into her pussy to get her nice and slick again for my cock.

My dick is so hard that I feel dizzy when I get back to my feet. But thankfully, Isobel takes over, her hands gripping the front of my jeans and trembling as she pops the button and lowers the zipper. Then, she's pushing the denim down, along with my boxer briefs. When they reach my knees, she lowers to hers to guide the fabric the rest of the way. After assisting with the removal of my shoes and the clothes, Isobel's fist wraps around my cock and then her lips seal around the crown. She licks and sucks me down her throat enough times to make me speak an unknown language.

Finally, when I can't take another second of her mouth, I pull her up off the floor. As soon as I hook my arms around her ass to lift her legs, she wraps them around me, and then our bodies are lined up perfectly. With her back braced against the door, I push forward, easing inside of her pussy that's so hot it burns me up in the best possible way.

"Oh wow," Isobel gasps when I'm fully sheathed in her and have to give us both a moment to adjust. "Best decision ever," she says, her eyes shut tight and head thrown back. She's so fucking gorgeous, and somehow I get to be with her.

I refuse to dwell on how I came to be with her right now. Instead, I focus on driving my hips, pounding inside of Isobel's amazing body so hard and so deep, we may fuck our way right through the door like a battering ram.

"*Yesyesyes*," Isobel chants as her arms tighten around my neck, pulling me closer just as her pussy clamps down on my cock when she comes. Burying my face in her neck, I succumb to my own release, thrusting slowly into her as I savor every shudder from the ecstasy pumping through my veins.

"Holy shit," Isobel whispers. "I'm not sure...if I can feel my legs."

"Don't worry. I've got you," I assure her.

And once my own legs get some of their strength back, I carry her over to the bed and collapse down into it with her.

"Wow. That was...well worth breaking my rule for," she says as we both lie flat on our backs, staring up at the ceiling.

"Glad to hear that," I say.

"Do you think the guys in the living room heard us?"

"Everyone up and down the street probably heard us," I tell her with a chuckle.

"Yeah," she agrees with a long sigh. Silence passes between us, and then Isobel says, "Don't take this the wrong way, Sax, but it's hard for me to see how you fit in with the Savage Kings."

"Why do you say that?" I ask curiously as I roll to my side and prop my head up with my elbow to look at her.

Isobel shifts so that she's on her side facing me with her palm resting underneath her cheek. "You don't disagree that you're sort of an outcast?"

"No," I reply. "You're right. I don't fit in. Never have. How did you know?"

"Then why did you join them?" she asks softly without answering my question.

"You really want to know?"

"Yes," she responds. "Please?"

"I've never told anyone this, but years ago, all I wanted was to take the entire MC down," I admit to her.

"How did you go from gunning for them to joining them?" she questions with her eyebrows drawn together.

"Because I was wrong about them. The Savage Kings aren't saints, but they weren't the bad guys I thought they were."

"You even talk about them like you're an outsider, not someone who is a member," she points out.

"Maybe that's because I've never felt like I belong, not really."

"But you feel like you owe them?"

Lowering my voice, I say, "Yeah. Even if April didn't feel the same way about me, I cared about her and was devastated when she died. I wanted someone to pay for taking her life, so I did something stupid – I become an informant for the DEA to try and bust the people who were responsible."

"And that *wasn't* the Savage Kings," she states.

"Nope. It was a bunch of idiot Aryans selling the tainted drugs that were killing people, not the Kings. In fact, the Kings actually shut down the people who were dealing, got their shit off the streets and probably saved lives. The club doesn't allow hard drugs in their town, so I was wrong."

"Did you tell the club once you realized your mistake?" Isobel asks.

"No. I've never said a word to anyone." Needing to touch her skin, I reach over and grasp her naked hip, then rub circles over it with my thumb. "If they found out...well, rats never get a pass in the MC."

"Not that I'm all that familiar with the terminology, but it doesn't sound like you were a rat," she says when she reaches over to stroke her palm over my arm and then up to April's promise ring hanging from my chain necklace.

"I was. I am," I say. "Loyalty is everything to the Savage Kings. I'm still trying to earn the trust they've put in me even though they shouldn't have."

"Nothing good ever comes from lying," she remarks, and my circling thumb on her hip freezes because she's right and I've been lying to her from the beginning.

"I know that," I reply. "But sometimes lying is unavoidable to protect the people you care about."

"Protecting them at what cost to yourself?" she asks.

"I don't mind being tied to the club. The MC is all I have now. They're all I've had for ten years. I couldn't go back to school or get a regular job. My parents didn't understand my decision to drop out of college and give up my football scholarship, so they were pissed at me and we grew apart. The club was the distraction I needed at the time, which is why I decided to stick with it."

"And you felt like you owed it to them after your perceived betrayal?" Isobel questions.

"Yeah, maybe that was a little part of why I patched in too."

After that statement, Isobel scoots over and cuddles up to me. It's nice just laying here with her, holding her in the silence. I feel lighter after telling her the truth, finally getting it off of my chest. Could I tell her the truth about everything and hope she understands what's at stake?

Before I can make a decision, Isobel asks, "What time is it?"

I have to let her go to get up to grab my phone from my jeans and check. "Almost six," I tell her when I find the device.

"I need to go check on Cooper," she says as she scoots to the edge of the bed. "Oh, but first I need a quick shower and change of clothes."

"I'll get dressed and then bring your things inside," I tell her when I pull on my jeans.

"Thanks," she says, flashing me a smile as she watches me get dressed with obvious appreciation in her eyes. The look she's giving me is nearly enough to make me hard again.

"You're kind of amazing, you know that?" I tell her.

"Oh, that's just those endorphins talking," she responds.

"The endorphins don't have anything to do with me wanting to kiss you a million times for helping my friend."

"In that case, I'll take you up on that offer after my shower and check-up."

"Deal," I agree with a smile.

AFTER I BRING in Isobel's guitar case and luggage, she takes off to the shower. Since there's nothing else to do at the moment, I lay back down in bed and wait for her to return to me.

Maybe she's on to something about the orgasms causing addiction, because I already need her again.

At first, when I saw her the other night in the bar, she was irresistible. I wanted her before she spoke a word to me just because she was gorgeous and had the voice of an angel.

Now, I just want to be with her, to get to know her better, to keep her. The more time we spend together, the closer we get.

If Isobel ever finds out that we met because of her father, though, she would never forgive me.

I hate that asshole so much, not just for blackmailing me and the guys, but for forcing me to involve her. It's not fair to Isobel. She's so sweet and kind, and here I am, sleeping with her and trying to figure out how to keep her around long enough to convince her to go back to nursing and make amends with her father.

The problem is, she sees too much. She took one look at me and the rest of the Savage Kings and knew I didn't belong. How am I supposed to keep manipulating her without her noticing?

Somehow, someway I need to convince her to do what her father wants.

"So, I had an idea!" Isobel says when she bursts back into the room, hair wet and fully dressed, interrupting my inner musings.

"Oh yeah?" I ask as I sit up and throw my legs over the side of the bed.

"The guys are all cranky and upset. They need some comfort food; and since Cooper seems stable, just sleeping things off for now, I can cook for them!"

"You're gonna cook for us?" I ask.

"Yeah. Who else will if I don't?" she questions.

"Well, there's always fast food," I point out. "We're grown men. We can fend for ourselves. Or send Cedric out."

Pulling out her tiny pink notepad and pen from her purse, she says, "I'm making a list, and then I'm going to the store. It'll be a great morale boost."

"Fine, but I'm going with you," I tell her.

Unfortunately, a few minutes later when we walk out of the bedroom, Torin's voice booms from the dining room, calling for a meeting.

"Just a second," I tell Isobel, leaving her at the back door so I can go talk to Torin. "Hey, man, I was about to head out with Isobel to grab some groceries," I tell him as everyone starts gathering around.

"Send Cedric with her," our president says. "Jade is calling to give us an update, so we need you here in case we need to take a vote."

"I don't know..." I start.

"The prospect can watch her back," Torin assures me. Since he's already wound tight, I doubt he's going to bend on this. Isobel and Cedric could probably go and get back by the time we adjourn, so I cave.

"Fine. Just give me a second," I tell our president before I grab Isobel's hand and pull her out the back. "I need to stay for a meeting. Do you think you'll be okay going with Cedric?"

"Yeah, sure," she says without hesitation, just like I predicted. Isobel's a tough girl who doesn't scare easily.

"He's probably hanging around outside," I say. And just as I thought, we find the kid leaning his back against the side of the van with his head bent over the phone in his hand.

"Just playing Tetris on my flip phone. No one can track me," Cedric tells me in a rush when he sees us approaching and straightens up.

"It's fine," I reply. "But I need you to put the phone away and go with Isobel to the grocery store. You mind?"

"No, sir," he answers, slipping the flip phone into his baggy jeans front pocket.

"Good. Watch her back and your own," I tell him. "And take off your cut."

"What?" he asks, reaching up to sweep the front of his thick black hair straight back and out of his eyes.

"Take off your cut and leave it here before you go," I clarify.

"Wait, is this a test?" he asks, looking between me and Isobel.

"A test?"

"Yeah, you know," he replies. "Like if I take off my cut, I fail. But if I don't do what you told me to do, I fail...less?"

"No, dickhead. This is not a test," I assure him. "There are people out there taking out Savage Kings' establishments. I don't want you drawing any attention to yourself right now. Got it?" I ask. I hate to get angry at the kid, but that's part of being a prospect, building up your confidence and growing a spine so that by the time you earn your patch, you won't let anyone speak down to you again.

"Oh, okay," Cedric says. He still hesitates a few more seconds before he finally slips his arms out of his cut and hands it to me.

"Good. Thank you," I tell him as I take the leather. "You'll get it back as long as you bring her back to me in one piece. If anything happens to her, I'll take it out on you five times over. Understood?"

"Yes, sir," he agrees with a nod before he opens the driver side of the van and climbs inside.

"A little harsh there, Sax," Isobel turns to me and says.

"We have to put the prospects through their paces, see if they have what it takes. It's tradition," I assure her. "Eventually, he'll stop letting us treat him like a dog and he'll get his patch."

"So it really is all just a test?" she asks me with a grin.

"Sort of," I agree with my own smile before wrapping my arm around her waist to pull her to me and cover her curved lips with mine. "Be careful. Have Cedric call me if anything comes up."

"We'll be fine," she says. "Now go, they're probably ready to start the meeting or whatever."

"Okay," I say as I reluctantly make my feet start back to the house, even though I would rather be going with Isobel. It's not safe for anyone to leave the group until we find out who is behind the attacks, but she's right and a good meal is what the guys need.

The van pulls away, and then I slip back inside and stand in the corner of the dining room since all six of the chairs are taken.

"Now that we're all here," Torin starts from his seat at the head of the table and then winces. "Except for Coop. I'm gonna call Jade and put her on speaker."

He gets her on the line and then pushes the speaker button and lays his phone down in the middle of the table.

"Hey, guys. Sorry you're dealing with all of this shit today," Jade says. "We still haven't had any luck tracking down family members of Jenna Higgins. None of the other dancers seem to know much about her. They all said she's only been at Avalon for a few weeks. Can you try to get more information from Cooper?"

"Ah, yeah," Torin responds. "But it may be tomorrow. He's had some hearing loss and been pretty out of it. Sax's nurse gave him something to help him relax and now he's sleeping."

"Okay, well, just tell me if you find out anything else. Maybe Reece can do some digging?"

"Sure," Reece agrees. "Do you have a date of birth?"

"Yeah, it's December fifth, nineteen-ninety-nine."

"I'll let you know what I can find."

"Thanks," Jade says. "As far as who is responsible, we still don't have any answers for you, which I know is frustrating. But I think you're doing the right thing, laying low. My deputies haven't seen anyone suspicious at the clubhouse or the Jolly Roger, but I'll keep them posted just in case."

"Can you give us any updates on the explosives?" War asks.

"The ATF has taken over, as you probably guessed, and they're not telling us much other than that the bombs were homemade with remote triggers, so we're probably dealing with a group that has a military background. Most of the homemade shit usually doesn't even detonate, much less work with a long-distance remote."

"That's a good point," Torin says. "Anything else?"

"The DEA is looking for you guys," Jade informs us. "Agent Wesley is acting like he just wants to sit down and talk about potential suspects, but I don't trust him. If you point him in the direction of suspects and the feds find them first, they could provide incriminating evidence against the Kings in exchange for a deal."

"Exactly," Chase says. "Fuck that. We're sitting tight and don't have anything to say to anyone."

"You'd be smart to get a lawyer."

"Ah, yeah, we sort of know one," Torin replies.

"The woman who was looking for Cooper?" Jade asks.

"Yeah, we've hired the firm she works for in the past, but I don't recall if she worked personally on any of the cases. Either way, she seems to have a relationship with Coop, so that could help us."

"Or it could be seen as a conflict," Jade points out. "Maybe you should get her to refer you to someone else in her firm. That way she can still keep you in the loop, but it puts some distance between her and the MC."

"Good idea," Torin agrees. "Anything else we need to know?"

"I'll have the incident reports for both buildings tomorrow so you can get them to your insurance company, and they can get to work on the claims," Jade tells us. "Do you plan to rebuild?"

"We're going to vote on that as soon as we hang up," Chase tells his step-sister.

"Sorry. None of my business. I'll be in touch when I find out more," she says and then ends the call.

"So?" Torin asks as he picks up his phone and glances around the room. "What does everyone think about rebuilding?"

"Yes to both," Dalton speaks up and says first. "Avalon is our biggest money maker and Gabe's tattoo shop is a big draw for tourists. Everyone wants to get inked by a Savage King."

"Thanks man," Gabe says with a nod in his direction.

"Yes to both," Abe answers. "You can never go wrong with a titty bar, and the shop is everything to my baby brother."

"Yes to both," Chase agrees. "In fact, Gabe, what do you say about a bigger building so that you could bring in a few more artists?"

"Hell yes," Gabe replies. "I would love the help, and I think we could triple the revenue with two more artists taking walk-ins since I'm usually booked up."

"That's a damn good idea," Torin says. "And if we have to rebuild anyway, we can have a contractor add the space for more chairs. All in favor?" he asks, and everyone answers in agreement. "Anyone opposed to the rebuild of Avalon?"

"Maybe there's room for improvement in the rebuild of Avalon too," I suggest.

"How so?" Chase questions.

"Well, you would have to talk to the dancers, but aren't virtual shows sort of hot right now?"

"Virtual shows?" War repeats, his brow wrinkled in confusion.

"Do you honestly never look at porn online?" Miles asks the club's father figure.

"Why do I need porn when I have a gorgeous woman in my bed?" War throws back, making Miles roll his eyes.

"Anyway," Reece says. "I think what Sax is referring to is the type of live porn when guys sign on to watch hot girls take off their clothes and...touch themselves while the audience watches."

"Exactly," I say. "It's not much of a stretch from stripping, right? Maybe even better for the dancers because they don't have to deal with the men getting handsy in private rooms or whatever. I bet we could build a few apartments over top of the new Avalon for production."

"That's pretty brilliant," Chase says. "And those sites charge by monthly memberships, right? If we had a few thousand subscribers for, say, five girls, we could have a shitload of new profits coming in. The only expenses would be to pay the women and set up the tech, which I'm sure Reece could do with his hands tied behind his back."

"Easily," Reece responds. "I'd need a server room with some hardcore firewalls and shit. Then we'd be in business upstairs and downstairs."

"Sounds like we can make the best out of a fucked-up situation," Maddox concludes.

"We'll cut out a percentage of the new Avalon's profits for Jenna's family," Torin says. "It's the least we can do for them since she died in our club."

"Agreed," Chase says, followed by everyone else's approval.

"As soon as we get everything settled with the insurance company, we'll have a contractor start rebuilding," Torin assures us. "We'll all feel the hit on our next quarterly payout, but we'll get through it. Just be patient, not only with the money side of things but with vengeance as well. We did what we had to do with the Russians; but if this is them hitting us back, we'll have to be careful going forward. No more innocents are going to die on my watch."

"Amen, brother. At least shit can't get any worse than this, but the Kings will always endure," War mutters, echoing everyone's sentiment.

And as the solemn mood fills the room, I can't help but think that they have no idea just how worse things can get for them thanks to the evidence the governor is holding over my head.

CHAPTER SIXTEEN

Sax

"I bought you something," Isobel whispers from behind me as I finish washing up the dinner dishes at the kitchen sink.

"You bought me something? Wasn't cooking dinner for all of us enough?" I ask.

"It's not much," she says. Wrapping both of her hands around my waist to rub their way up the front of my shirt, she says, "I'll be in bed with it when you finish up here," before she walks away.

Never in all my life have I washed dishes as fast as I did then. In fact, tomorrow I'll probably need to rewash them. We really need to get a dishwasher put in here.

When I slip into our room a few moments later, I'm only a little disappointed to find Isobel sitting up in bed, still wearing her clothes.

"You thought I would be naked, didn't you?" she asks with a grin.

"Maybe."

"I'll be naked soon enough," she promises, which is all it takes for my cock to start swelling down my jean leg.

"That's good to know," I tell her as I flop down on the mattress next to her on my side.

"Are you ready for your present?" she asks excitedly.

"Yes."

Reaching beside her on the nightstand, she grabs a tiny blue notebook with matching pen that looks similar to her pink one.

"This is *your* bucket list," she says when she places it in front of me on the bed. "Now you have one so you can start putting down all the things you want to do or see before you die."

"Thank you," I tell her, sitting up to place a kiss on her cheek.

Positioning my back against the headboard, I pull the pen free and open up the notebook to the first blank page.

"Well, I wanted to kiss you, so that's one I can check off," I say as I scribble "Kiss Isobel" on the first line and put a check mark beside of it. "Then I went skinny dipping, which is something I had never done before but always wanted to do," I add, checking it off as well.

"Now add 'travel around the world on your boat,'" Isobel instructs, so I jot it down. "What else?" she asks.

"I'll need some time to think about it."

"There must be some ideas on your mind, no matter how farfetched or impossible or silly. Just write it down, Sax. Then find a way to make time to do it!"

"Okay," I reply with a heavy exhale before I write down the thing I've wanted to do since I was a kid.

Isobel tilts her head to the side to read it aloud. *"Find a shipwreck.* You mean like pirate treasure?" she asks with a smile.

"Not to try to find gold and get rich or whatever, but just to study it. I think it would be pretty cool to find a piece of history at the bottom of the ocean."

"Oh, I get it," Isobel says. "You're a closeted history dork."

"No, I'm not," I scoff indignantly, causing her to giggle. Finally, I admit the truth. "Okay, so maybe I am a little bit."

"That's sort of adorable," she says. "I knew you weren't cut out to be a Savage King. You want to be a savage pirate instead." A giggle escapes her curved lips before she adds, "You already have the boat and one-eyed cat. Oh! You should totally get a tiny little black patch for Willy to wear!"

"You think you're hilarious, don't you?" I tease right before I launch myself at her, pulling her back down on the mattress and pinning her underneath me while I squeeze her sides, tickling the shit out of her.

"Stop! Stop! Truce, Captain! Please!" Isobel squirms and laughs.

"Thank you," I tell her when I finally relent, hovering over top of her. "I'll try to check off as many items on my bucket list as possible. And now I know not to let *anyone* ever read it," I joke before I steal a kiss from her lips. And then another until we're both naked and losing ourselves in each other's bodies.

CHAPTER SEVENTEEN

Isobel

The next morning, as soon as I wake up, I slip quietly into Cooper's room to see how he's doing. From the moment my palm touches his forehead, I can tell he has a fever.

"C-cold," he stammers because he's also shivering.

"Sorry, but no more blankets for you until your fever comes down," I say to him, even though he probably can't hear me.

Grabbing the thermometer from the top of the dresser, I sit on the edge of the mattress and ease the device underneath his armpit to see just how high it's gone since my last check around four a.m. At that time, it had been a perfect ninety-eight point eight, so I had slipped back into bed with Sax.

Cooper barely notices what I'm doing with his teeth chattering so hard and the rest of his body shuddering.

Finally the low beep on the thermometer tells me it's finished, and I cringe at the result. His temperature is now a hundred and one underneath his arm, which is usually one degree lower than the actual temp.

I hurry into the bedroom Sax and I slept in last night to tell him the bad news.

"Sax," I say when I'm standing next to his side of the bed and giving his bare shoulder a shake. "Hey, Sax. Cooper has a fever."

"Shit," his groggy voice grumbles before his eyes even open. "High?"

"High enough," I reply as he peeks at me with one blue eye. "We can try giving him some Tylenol and see if that will bring it down, but it's worrisome either way. His body is trying to fight an infection."

"Yeah, let's hope the Tylenol works," Sax agrees.

"Can you help me sit Cooper up so he can swallow a few pills? He's shivering and looks pretty miserable."

"Ah, yeah, of course," Sax says as he pushes himself up in the bed. "Let me throw on my clothes and I'll meet you in his room."

"I'll go grab the bottle from the kitchen cabinet," I say since I remember seeing a few of the standard meds in there yesterday.

It's not easy to get Cooper alert enough to take the pills, but we finally get him to swallow two extra strength Tylenol with a sip of water before he passes out again.

"Why is he so..." Sax asks as we stand over his friend. "Out of it."

"His body is trying to recover from a serious trauma. Hopefully it's just the high fever making him weak and sleepy, but for all we know he could have internal injuries. Without a CT or MRI, there's no way to know."

"You think we need to take him to the hospital?" Sax asks.

"Yes, but I understand the reason you can't," I assure him. "For now we can attribute his condition to the fever, but we may need to find something stronger than Tylenol if it doesn't come down soon."

"Yeah, okay," Sax agrees. "What do we do now?"

"Wait," I tell him. "That's all we can do. Wait and let him rest and recover. He's lucky to be alive. If he can survive a building blowing up, he'll be able to overcome these injuries."

Sax

WHILE WAITING to see if Coop's meds work, I join the guys in the living room to watch a baseball game on television. Despite the delicious meal Isobel made yesterday for us, today the guys are brooding, worried about Cooper's rising temp and missing their women. The silence and tension is so thick in the room that you could cut it. So, when I see Isobel walk out the back door with her guitar in her hands, I get up and follow her.

She's already seated on one of the steps, strumming her pick over the strings when I walk outside.

"Bored?" I ask her when I sit down beside her.

"No, not at all," she replies with a smile. "I enjoy the downtime. But I need a distraction to keep myself from worrying unnecessarily about Cooper's fever."

"You're worried about him?" I ask in surprise.

"Well, yeah. He's my patient, and a fever means infection," Isobel responds. "If his body can't fight it..."

"We'll need something strong and may have to cave and take him to the hospital?" I finish.

"Yeah," she agrees. "And I know that would make everything more complicated when the guys are already tense enough as it is, concerned for Cooper and upset about who is responsible."

"Well, let's just pray the fever comes down," I say on a sigh.

Isobel's fingers move over the guitar strings as she starts playing a somewhat familiar tune.

"Some people don't believe it, but I think music is good for the soul," she tells me. "Studies even show that it can have a positive effect on the sick when the songs are relaxing and familiar."

"Really?" I reply since I've never thought about music as a remedy to ailments.

"Sure," Isobel says. "Music can reduce anxiety, help depression, lower your heart rate and blood pressure. There's a reason so many people enjoy hearing their favorite songs over and over again. Listening to music releases dopamine, which lifts your mood. Everyone knows a song that can lift you up every time you hear it."

"Oh, yeah?" I ask. "Like what?"

Instead of telling me a song title, Isobel plays the tune on her guitar until I catch on. "Walking on Sunshine, right?" I guess, then I remember the jackass at her father's house mentioning it. Daniel said Isobel would sing it to their patients to calm them down and it always worked.

"Who can listen to this song and not find themselves just a little bit happier after it's over?" she says as she plays the last cord.

"That's very true," I agree. "Even if it's not exactly my style, it's still uplifting."

"So what is your style?" Isobel asks.

"I don't know, I listen to rock mostly. Guys like Tom Petty. I've got a bunch of his CDs on the boat."

Isobel adjusts her grip on the neck of her guitar, and a moment later begins strumming "American Girl". As she settles into the rhythm, she begins to sing the familiar lyrics while I sit and stare at her, mesmerized.

"Who else do you like?" she smiles at me as she finishes the song with a flourish a few minutes later.

"I...Isobel, that was awesome," I tell her. "Another singer I like? Man, I don't know, maybe Bruce Springsteen?" I stammer. I'm struck speechless when she immediately launches into another song, "Born to Run". I stare at her slack-jawed, still unable to find any words when she finishes the song.

"How do you do that?" I finally manage to ask her. "How do you just know the chords and lyrics off the top of your head?" I ask her in total awe. I knew she was talented after seeing her on stage, but now she's blowing my mind.

Lifting one of her shoulders and letting if fall, she says, "Music comes as naturally to me as breathing."

"Then why not make a career out of it, Iz?" I ask.

"Because no one sucks the soul out of music more than record labels. Musicians are squeezed for every penny so that the greedy corporate assholes can get richer. I want more freedom, not less, even if I do love to sing and play."

"I, ah, I guess that makes sense," I tell her. Isobel refuses to be tied down by anything or anyone. And here I am, trying to do just that to her.

"I play in the bars I want and don't ask for a dime," she says. "I do it because I want to and I enjoy it, not to try and profit off of something I love."

"I get it," I say honestly. Slipping my hand up underneath the back of her shirt, I lean over to kiss her cheek and then move my lips down to her neck, over her ear. "Will you play something else for me?" I ask.

"Any requests?" she asks as she shivers.

"Lady's choice," I reply, nipping at her neck with my teeth before I move away.

"Well, in that case," she says as she starts to strum the tune. It's not a song I recognize right away, although the lyrics start out a little harsh. When she gets to the chorus of Jewell's "Who Will Save Your Soul" the hairs on my arms stand up, and not in the same way as they did the first time I heard Isobel singing on stage. No, this time, the song is too accusatory because I've been lying to her and I feel wretched for it.

Isobel was wrong. Sometimes songs can make a person feel worse than they already felt, not better.

I'm so lost in my own thoughts, drowning in my sea of guilt, that I don't even notice the back door is open until there's a round of applause and even a few whistles when Isobel stops playing.

"She's a nurse, she cooks, *and* she sings like an angel?" Dalton says. "You better put a ring on her finger and lock that shit down now, Sax," he adds, reaching down to slap my shoulder.

"Thank you, boys," Isobel says when she stands up with her guitar still slung over her shoulder to turn around and take a bow.

"Do you know any nineties bands, Alice in Chains or Pearl Jam?" Abe asks.

Shaking myself out of my own dark thoughts, I tell the guys, "She's like a human jukebox. Name a song and she can play it."

"No way," Maddox says. "How about playing some Skynyrd?"

For the next hour, Isobel gives the Savage Kings their own private concert. And just one look at all their faces and I can see *exactly* what she means about music relaxing people. Everyone's been tense and on edge since the bombings yesterday and while we wait for Cooper to get better. Then, Isobel worked her magic on them once again, this time with music instead of food, and there's an entire shift in the mood around the house for the rest of the night.

She's so fucking amazing, practically glowing with warmth and goodness. And I'm an asshole; because to save the Kings, I'm going to have to snuff out some of that light.

CHAPTER EIGHTEEN

Sax

By morning, Cooper's temperature is higher, not lower, so we call a group meeting in the kitchen.

"We're gonna have to get him a hospital strength antibiotic," Isobel tells us. "A tetanus shot wouldn't hurt either since we don't know if he's had one in the past ten years. There was a lot of random debris lodged in his wounds."

"Where do we get those kinds of things? A pharmacy?" Torin asks.

"We can't get either from a pharmacy without a prescription or taking him there for the shot," Isobel says. "A local hospital is our best bet. They're busier with more staff running around, so it will be easier to steal from them than a pharmacy."

"Okay, I'll go," I volunteer.

"No, Sax," she objects. "You won't know where or how to get in the medicine machines. I did an internship at the hospital and I can blend in."

We all stare silently at her, likely thinking the same thing – she *won't* blend in.

"I'll dye my hair back to brown and throw on some scrubs. Trust me, guys, I can do this."

"Fine, but I'm going with you," I tell her.

"Okay, if you insist," she agrees. "If someone can get me the hair dye and scrubs, we can go tonight. Hospital ERs get flooded on the weekends when doctor offices are closed, especially after dark when people start drinking and doing idiotic shit."

"I'll go get both of those things for you right now," Cedric volunteers. Probably because he knows we would likely send him out anyway since he's a prospect.

And sure enough, a few hours later, Isobel comes out of the bathroom looking so...normal. I can't believe how differently she looks with her hair back to its natural color, or at least a hair color found in nature. She's now the innocent girl her father so desperately wants her to be.

"I prefer the blue hair," I tell her as I pick up a silky strand hanging beside her face and let it slide through my fingers.

"Good, because it's going back to turquoise and purple as soon as we get this done," she promises.

Despite how natural she looks, I realize that this girl isn't the real Isobel. She once told her father that the hair and leather dress were a costume, a way to hide the fact that she's the governor's daughter. Now I know she was lying. Her wild hair and lifestyle are who she really is, who she wants to be. And I don't want to be the one to ask her to change for her father. But I have to try. There's too much on the line.

Besides, Isobel only needs to go back to her normal life for a few months.

Or so I tell myself before I remember something the governor said to me the first day we met when he came to my cell.

He has presidential ambitions.

He doesn't need Isobel to fit into his mold for a few months. I bet he's going to try and force her to be someone she's not for years.

CHAPTER NINETEEN

Isobel

"I 'll stay nearby and create a distraction in case someone catches you," Sax promises me after he kills the engine on his bike right outside the crowded ER parking lot. First, we had to make a quick stop at his boat to feed his cat, which was pretty freaking sweet.

"Just be patient," I tell him. "First, I'll need to snatch someone's employee access card, and then I'll have to watch nurses open the machines here a few times before I give it a try."

"Okay," he agrees. "Be careful, and good luck," he adds before giving me a quick kiss on the lips. "I'll be in the waiting room. If you get into trouble, I'll raise a ruckus while you get out."

Ever since this afternoon when I dyed my hair, Sax has been acting off. I give him one more quick kiss, then walk briskly into the main entrance near the emergency room. Whatever is bugging him will have to wait, and I force myself to put it out of my mind as I walk through check-in and down the corridors into the bowels of the hospital.

The trick to doing anything shady, as I've learned through trial and error, is to always move confidently and act like you belong. The emergency room is wild and rocking tonight, with a cacophony of groans, shrieks, and raised voices echoing down the halls as I scan doorways, looking for one particular sign. Doctors in white coats and all sorts of nurses, aides, and staff in scrubs swirl past me as I roam, soon stumbling upon a back hall with the exact door I needed.

"On-Call Room," I whisper. "Bingo!" I add as I lean on the wall just outside the door, doing my best to paste a worried expression on my face. While the hallway is clear, I surreptitiously attempt to open the door, but it's locked, as I expected. There's a small number pad over the handle, but I leave it alone for now. Only a few moments later I hear footsteps approaching, and when a man in a white coat appears around the corner reading a tablet, I quickly move to intercept him.

"Dr. Nelson!" I call out as I read his nametag. "Thank goodness you came along," I gush with my most charming smile. "I'm a new intern, and this is my first rotation on the ER, and for the life of me I can't remember the code to the lounge. I left my ID in there earlier..." I trail off with a helpless wide-eyed gaze, pleading for his assistance.

"You aren't the first, and you won't be the last," Dr. Nelson smiles at me, obviously smitten. "Heck, I had to write the codes down on my forearm for two weeks for all the doors in this place." Walking over to the door, he punches a code into the pad, and cracks the door for me. "Shhh!" he mimes with a finger to his lips as he uses his foot to prop open the door. "Don't wake the others or there will be hell to pay. Good luck, doctor...?"

"Wrigley," I volunteer in a whisper. "Thank you so much, Dr. Nelson. I'll see you around later, I'm sure!" I duck into the on-call room and quickly shut the door behind me, just in case my new friend had any ideas about following me.

Glancing around, I can see several figures curled up in the bunks in the shadows of the room. Interns are always run into the ground, so I breathe a small sigh of relief as I move deeper into the room. I know everyone in here could probably sleep through the apocalypse, so I'm not too worried about anyone noticing me. It only takes me one lap around the room to spot what I need. One of the interns is lying flat on her back, arm over her eyes, snoring softly with her ID clipped perfectly to the breast of her scrubs. With one deft movement, I lift it free, not even interrupting her breathing. If the rest of my plan holds up, I will be out of here before my victim ever wakes.

I ease back out of the on-call room with my newfound ID clipped to my scrubs, then dash back through the hallways towards the emergency room. I'm lucky that I don't need to steal any 'hard' drugs, as the issues Cooper is having should only require antibiotics. Once I'm near the emergency room, I quickly locate a supply closet and use the ID badge to swipe my way inside.

Inside, I grab a clean pair of navy-blue scrubs that are folded and stacked just inside the door, not even looking to see what size they are. I don't need them to wear, but to hide the rest of my contraband. I quickly wrap up two IV kits as well as a bag of saline and electrolytes. Once I've secured the bundle under my arm, I leave the closet and head into the ER's patient exam rooms.

I pause briefly outside each room to scan the patient's charts, picking up each one and reading over it brazenly, as though I'm their treating physician. None of the nurses hustling through the ER stop to even glance at me; and in only a few minutes, I've found the room that I need.

"How are you doing, Mr. Wilkinson?" I ask as I walk into the room of an elderly gentleman who, according to his chart, is presenting tonight for suspicion of pneumonia.

"Doctor?" Mr. Wilkinson wheezes. "Thought you were just in here a moment ago. I must have nodded off there for a bit. I'm holding up all right, still just waiting for a room to open up. Looks like I'll be staying a few days."

"Well, we're going to take excellent care of you, sir," I reassure him as I check the medications on his IV pole. One bag of antibiotics is already flowing into him, but the nurses were good enough to prep a second bag of Zithromax and leave it hanging on standby on the pole. "Everything looks good here," I add for the patient as I quickly add the secondary bag to my stash. "But if you need anything at all, don't hesitate to call the nurse, okay?"

"Thanks again, doctor," Mr. Wilkinson says as he shifts to a more comfortable position in the bed. With a small sigh of relief, I leave the room, trying unsuccessfully to squash the spike of guilt I feel at stealing the antibiotic from that poor old man. I have no doubt that it will be chalked up to a simple error and replaced, but I still can't help feeling ashamed. Consoling myself with the knowledge that I'm doing this to help Cooper, I rejoin the crowd of people in the emergency room waiting area. I spot Sax immediately; and once I give him a small nod, he stands up and moves towards the exit doors.

While I'm in the midst of the crowd milling near the check-in desk, I drop the ID card I had pilfered, and then duck through the sliding doors that seem to be perpetually stuck open with all of the people crowding inside.

"You have any problems?" Sax asks me once we're a safe distance away in the parking lot.

"No, thankfully they're so busy that no one even glanced twice at me. God, that was nerve-wracking, though. I haven't stolen anything since I was a teenager and nabbed a candy bar from the gas station. Now I remember why I never added 'stealing' to my bucket list. I never want to do that again!"

"I'm sorry I had to ask you to help with this," Sax says as we reach his motorcycle. "I can't tell you how much this means to me and to my crew. We might have put a lot of people in danger if Cooper had to be admitted. You've done something good here, even though I know it must not feel like it. I can't believe how smooth you were in there; you were in and out in under thirty minutes."

"Come on, Captain, point this ship towards the shore," I quip as I get my helmet on and secure my bundle in his saddlebags. I'm more pleased by his compliment than I care to concede, and I can admit to myself that it feels good to be truly helping someone again. "We'll see if this was worth it once Cooper starts to recover."

CHAPTER TWENTY

Isobel

My footsteps halt when I walk into the bedroom and find Cooper sitting up on the edge of the mattress. "Oh my God. You're wide awake!" I say in surprise.

"What?" he shouts at me, obviously unable to hear the volume of his own voice. Reaching up slowly, like his arms are heavy, he scratches the back of his matted bed head and asks, "Who the hell are you?" Before I can try to answer, he drops his arm back to his side and says, "Actually, I don't care. Just tell me where I can take a piss."

Grabbing his elbow, I turn his arm over and sigh helplessly as I see where he has pulled out the IV I inserted last night. "Well, the good news is that you at least got all the fluids in your veins before you ripped everything out," I tell him. He doesn't respond, so I help him to his feet and guide him out of the room to the bathroom in the hallway.

As soon as he shuts himself inside, I yell, "Guys! Cooper's awake!" even though some are probably still sleeping.

Half-naked bikers appear from every doorway within seconds, completely surrounding me before they filter into the room Cooper's been sleeping in.

"Where is he?" Torin asks.

"Bathroom," I reply with a nod of my head toward the only closed door.

"How's his temperature today?" Sax asks.

"Don't know. He was up and out of bed before I could check it. But I touched his arm, and he didn't feel warm. The fact that he's up is a good sign, and now may be the best time to get some pen and paper to tell him about his hearing."

"Good idea," Chase agrees. "Anyone have any paper or a pen?"

"I do," I say, and then I hurry back into our room to fish my bucket list notebook and pen out of my bag. Flipping to a blank page when I return to the hallway, I ask the guys, "Should I start by telling him that there was an explosion and your eardrums blew so he may not be able to hear us?"

"That works," Torin agrees. "Then we'll go from there."

The toilet flushes, sink comes on, and then a few minutes later the bathroom door opens. Cooper physically startles when he sees everyone gathered around because he didn't hear us talking in the hallway.

"What are you all doing here?" he asks.

"Let's get him back to bed before we get into the details," I suggest.

"Huh?" Cooper shouts as War and Torin grab his elbows and steer him back into the room. "What's going on?" he asks. "Why won't anyone fucking answer me!" he shouts after he flops back down on the bed.

I offer him the notebook and then point to the words I wrote in it when we were in the hallway.

"Yeah, I remember the explosion," he says. "Who did it?"

The guys shrug their shoulders in the universal gesture for no idea, so that doesn't need to be written down.

"Shit, my eardrums are fucked. Is that why there's whooshing and ringing in them?" Cooper asks.

I nod, and then take back the notebook to write down that we need to take him to an audiologist now that he's feeling better before turning it around to show to him.

"Fine," he mutters after reading it. "Anything to make this stop – Wait, Jenna?" he asks, his pale, bluish-silver eyes widening in panic as he looks around the room.

For this response, I hand the notebook to Torin, the guy in charge. I feel like this is something he should 'hear' from one of his brothers.

As soon as Torin hands him the book with the words he wrote down on the page, Cooper groans and shakes his head as the notebook falls from his hands. "No! No, God, no!" he exclaims as his palms scrub down his face. "She has a kid...what about her kid?"

"Oh fuck," someone mutters since none of them apparently knew that bit of information.

"We need to get a name and address for her family," Torin says aloud as he picks up the notebook to probably write the same thing.

"No one has had any luck, but we'll keep trying," Sax offers.

"When we find them, see what they need, how much money for the funeral and any other expenses. We're gonna take care of her kid," Torin says as he pulls Cooper's hand from his face to show him the writing on the page. Instead of making him feel better, he falls apart and sobs. "It wasn't your fault," Torin says before he scribbles the sentence on the page and holds it up in front of his face. "It wasn't, okay?"

"Let's give him some time to process all of this on his own," I suggest. "Maybe someone can locate an audiologist in the area and call to get him an appointment ASAP since I'm not allowed to have a phone."

"I'll do it," War offers.

"Thanks, man," Torin says. "I'll stay here with him if you all want to give us some time…"

"We'll need to check his temperature soon and change his bandages," I tell him. "Let me know when you think he's ready."

"Thanks, Iz," Torin says, using my abbreviated nickname like he's finally accepting me into the group.

That's when it hits me that I only agreed to stay until Cooper was up and around, which is…today.

~

Sax

"Did you find out anything about her family?" Isobel asks when she joins me outside in the backyard after I made a few phone calls.

"No," I answer with a sigh. "Jade spoke to a few of the dancers, but none of them knew if her family is local or not. No one mentioned a kid, so she must have kept that to herself. Reece didn't have any luck either. There were no other Higgins in Durham where she's originally from. I just called the coroner's office, and they said no one has been in to claim her body, so either she has no family, or they don't know yet."

"Jesus," Isobel says. "Either way it's awful, especially since she has a child."

"We'll keep trying to track them down," he says. "Do you by chance have a laptop I could borrow?"

"Yeah, there's one in my bag, I just haven't used it for fear it would be confiscated too."

"I'll try to get your phone back," I tell her. "Torin's eased up and trusts you more now that you robbed a hospital to help Coop and he's back on his feet."

"Physically, maybe," she says. "He's still going to have to deal with the hearing issue and emotional turmoil. He's hurting bad, Sax."

"He blames himself for whatever reason. Jenna was his employee, and now he feels guilty that he couldn't save her."

"He shouldn't," Isobel says. "There was nothing he could've done to stop a bomb that someone else planted."

"Maybe not, but I get it," I tell her.

"Right, you *wrongly* blamed yourself when April died," she responds.

"Yeah, I got pissed at her for partying, getting high and seeing other guys. I should've done more to get her help, been around more. But I was pissed and pushed her away after I found out she slept with someone else."

"It wasn't your fault, Sax. Sometimes people do stupid things that they know they shouldn't, and any consequences fall solely on them."

I give a nod of agreement but don't have anything to say to that. April's death was partially my fault, and that's always how I'll see it. Isobel could never understand.

"I didn't exactly *quit* being a nurse," she tells me.

"What do you mean?" I ask.

"I got fired for showing up drunk or hungover from staying out at bars and clubs too late," she starts. "Danny knew, and he gave me more chances than I deserved. Honestly, I took advantage of the fact that we were friends and I was certain that he wouldn't fire me," she explains before she pushes her still brown hair behind her ear. "But then one day a parent smelled the alcohol on my breath and reported me *and* Danny to the medical board. I told them he didn't know anything about my drinking, so they took my license but let him keep his."

"Damn, Iz. That's awful," I say. I had no idea that's why she left nursing.

"I think deep down I wanted them to take my license all along, which is why I kept drinking to excess. I wanted to finally be free to do whatever I wanted."

"Why would you want to throw away the years it took to get your nursing degree and all if you didn't actually want it?" I ask her.

"When I was younger, I thought a career in nursing *was* what I wanted, to be able to help people like my mother. And then I got the results back from the genetic testing I did on a whim and learned the truth."

"The truth? About what?"

"My mother never had cancer like my father told me," Isobel says. "She had Huntington's disease, and he kept it from me."

"What's Huntington's again? I know I've heard of it before, but I don't remember the details," I tell her.

"It's a, ah, rare genetic condition that breaks down the nerves in a person's brain, which is why it's *always* fatal, eventually."

"Jesus."

"Children of Huntington's patients have a fifty percent chance of inheriting it," Isobel explains. "I have it."

"Hold on. You have Huntington's disease, like, right now?" I ask in disbelief, and she nods. She looks and seems so healthy! "Are you okay? What exactly does that mean?"

"I'm okay now, but I've already started showing symptoms – the occasionally twitching of fingers, hands and feet, the frequent clumsiness and dropping things, all of which means that over the next ten to fifteen years the nerves in my brain will deteriorate a little more each day until I'm no longer capable of caring for myself and the disease finally kills me."

"You can't be serious," I say. "You're perfectly healthy. There must be some sort of mistake..."

"There's no mistake, Sax! I only have maybe ten good years left. After that, I'll be bedridden until I can no longer speak or eat, and then I'll die."

"No. There has to be something doctors can do before it gets that bad."

"There are medicines to help with the symptoms, but there is no cure," she says with a shake of her head.

"Not yet, but maybe one day. You can't just give up hope, Iz."

"Sax, it's a rare disease. Not enough people have it to waste billions of dollars on research finding a cure. The only way to stop it is for those who have it to stop procreating."

"Wow," I say, still in a state of shock, unable to formulate any other words. So that's why she had her tubes tied, to make damn sure she doesn't pass the disease on to her kids.

"How ironic, right?" she asks. "I wanted to work with children, and then I find out that I can't even have any of my own," Isobel says sadly. "That's another reason that deep down I wanted to get out of pediatrics."

"You could...you could still have kids if you want them. There's a chance they wouldn't get it."

"I'm not willing to take that chance and condemn some poor kid to die in his or her forties!"

"What about adoption then?" I offer.

"No," she says without hesitation. "Any kids I have, my own or someone else's, will be destined to the same hell – to take care of me, to watch me fall apart."

"That's why you...this is why you have a bucket list," I say in understanding.

"The clock is ticking," Isobel replies. "Each day I get closer to the end when I won't be able to walk or talk or do the things I want to do."

"And your father knows this?" I ask in horror. "He knows that you have Huntington's and that your life will be cut short?"

"Of course," she answers. "He was the first person I told. I confronted him after I received my results and started digging into my mother's history. Do you know what he did?" she grits out.

I shake my head, unable to speak because I was trying to do what her father wanted, to keep her grounded, to stop her from living her life to the fullest, which is the least she deserves.

"My father printed my mother's obituary in the paper when I was ten to convince me and everyone else that she was gone. We had a memorial service for her!"

"She wasn't dead?" I ask.

"No! She didn't die until almost five years later! He hid her from me and the world in a nursing home because he said he didn't want me to see her like that – to see what *I* was going to have to endure in just a few decades! They had tested me when I was a kid and knew what would happen. He didn't want me to know that my life would end before I hit fifty."

"God, Isobel. I'm so...I'm so fucking sorry," I tell her honestly.

"You have nothing to apologize for," she replies with a small smile. "These last few days with you have been some of the best of my life. I hadn't realized just how isolated and alone I was before you came along. But now you know why I can't let myself get too close to you or anyone else."

I have to clear the emotion from my throat before I can ask, "And why exactly is that?"

"Because no one wants to be the man who has to feed and bathe his sick wife for years before losing her. Not even my own father, who I thought loved my mother, could do it. He tossed her into a home so someone else could care for her while he pretended she was dead and went on with his life."

Panic. All I feel inside me is a growing, suffocating panic as I feel her slipping away from me for good.

"I may have only known you for a few days, Iz, but I would do anything to spend every day of the rest of my life with you," I tell her honestly.

"Sax..." she starts.

"I'm serious," I say when I grab her hand. "Stay with me. Or let me go with you. I just don't want this to end yet."

"You don't know what you're saying. Ten years, Sax, that would be the most you get with me before I'll need around-the-clock care."

"Then let me have ten years with you. We'll make them count. They'll be amazing, I promise," I tell her.

When tears start to trickle down her cheeks, I pull her close to me, and she tilts her head up to kiss me. Her lips crush into mine, fierce and passionate, but I break away before she can distract me further.

"Is that a yes?" I ask her with a small smile.

Instead of answering, she launches herself at me, tangling her hands in my hair. "Take me to bed," she demands, her lips pressed directly to my ear.

As she grinds herself against me, I realize this is the only answer I'm going to get for now, and honestly, it's one that I'm happy to accept. She hasn't refused me, and her body is telling me everything that I need to know.

Well, everything that I need to know for the next hour.

.

CHAPTER TWENTY-ONE

Isobel

Sax and I are still tangled up in bed when a cell phone beeps yet again, snapping him out of a light doze. Torin gave me my phone back, finally, but I know by the tone that it's Sax's.

"Ugh, sorry, but I better grab that, baby," he mumbles, so I slide off of his chest.

"Anything important?" I ask, "Or can we stay here a bit longer?"

"It's Gabe," Sax says. "Him and Abe went out and got him a new kit. I mean his needle guns and inks, all that stuff. He says they're on their way back to the safehouse, and he'd be glad to do your tattoo, if you're still up for it. What do you say, want to hang out a little longer and get some ink?" Sax asks, excitement and hope lightening his tone. "I'd want you to stay a bit while it heals, make sure it doesn't need touching up or anything."

"Tell him I'd love that," I confirm with a smile. While I do want the tattoo to remember him, what we've had together, I know I still need to temper Sax's expectations. "It will be a beautiful way to remember the time we've had together. You really are the best, Sax. These last few days have been...well, they have been some of the best of my life."

"But you still won't stay, will you?" he asks, his voice tinged with disappointment and bitterness.

"I know how hard it is to understand," I tell him as I get up and begin dressing. "I want you to believe this, Sax. If there was any man that I would consider having near me while this disease progresses, any man that I would trust to care for me like a child, an invalid child...it would be you. But I promised myself a long time ago that I would never put anyone through that. No one. Ever."

"Isobel, listen," Sax protests, just as heavy footsteps can be heard out in the hall.

"Yo, you guys decent in there?" Gabe yells from outside the door. "I sent that text like half an hour ago. You ready for some ink?"

"Yes, come on in," I call out before Sax can say anything else. I'm still only in my t-shirt and a thong, but with the idea I have for the placement of my tattoo, that's the most appropriate thing to be wearing.

Gabe opens the door as Sax is fastening his jeans, first looking over to him before his gaze is drawn to my naked legs. "Whoa, hello there," Gabe snorts. "You sure you guys don't need a minute?"

"No," Sax grumbles as he collapses into a chair. "She's ready to go."

"I wanted to get the cherry blossom and a couple of butterflies up my hip, here," I tell Gabe, pointing out the area to him. "Should I just lie on the bed? Can you do it in here, you think?"

"Yeah, the light is good in here," Gabe confirms. "Lie down and I'll get my stuff out, then show you the stencil I worked up."

Once Gabe is prepared and has placed the stencil on my hip, Sax finally gets up from his seat and comes over to take a look. His stern face instantly softens as he looks at the design. "It's beautiful," he sighs. "Does it mean something special to you, Izzie, or is it just for the look?"

I'm so happy to see his mood lighten up that I answer right away, without realizing my answer might bother him. "I wanted the cherry blossoms and butterflies because they're both so ephemeral and short-lived. While beautiful, you have to appreciate them all the more because they're so fleeting."

After I explain my reasoning, I glance up from the stencil to see Sax's face. His eyes are shining as though he's fighting back tears, and his face is tight with barely controlled emotion. "You get to work, Gabe," he says in a thick voice. "I'm going to go get a drink. You want anything?"

"Water, please," Gabe says as he pulls a chair close to the bed and sits down.

"One for me, too, please," I add.

"Coming right up," Sax says with a sniff, swiping at his nose as he leaves the room.

"Didn't have him pegged as the sentimental type," Gabe snorts as he tests his tattoo gun, the tiny engine whining to life and almost drowning out his words.

"He's got some things buried really deep," I tell Gabe. "But there are treasures in those depths worth exploring."

"Well, cheers to you, Isobel," Gabe grins. "Always nice to meet someone else with the soul of an artist, especially among these barbarians. Now, you just relax, and I'll take good care of this for you."

Sax comes back a short time later with two bottles of water, which he places on the bedside table. Without making any comment, he goes back to sit on the other side of the room, making sure not to interrupt Gabe's concentration.

The tattoo is almost painless under his deft touch, the only pain coming when he drags his needle across my hip bone while etching a butterfly. It takes him less than three hours to complete the entire design, his hand never seeming to tire and his attention never wavering.

"That's it," Gabe tells me as he leans back and uses a clean rag to wipe the area gently a few more times. "I brought you a bottle of lotion to rub on it several times a day while it heals up, and you probably want to keep it covered the first day or so, unless you want it bleeding all over your clothes. You got any questions for me?"

"Gabe, it's beautiful!" I gush before I hop up from the bed and walk over to the mirror to see it better. "Thank you so much for doing this for me!"

"Thank you for all you've done for my boys, Cooper and Sax both," Gabe replies. "You've made both of them better, I think. I'm going to get on out of here; but if you have any trouble, Sax knows how to reach me, okay?"

"Thanks, brother," Sax says as he finally stands up and goes to open our bedroom door. He slaps Gabe on the shoulder as he leaves, then closes the door behind him.

I turn towards Sax, unable to hide my elation at how well the colors turned out. I quickly pull the t-shirt I was wearing over my head, so that I'm standing by the mirror in only my thong. "Tell me what you think, Captain. Do you approve? Personally, I love it!"

"I didn't think it was possible for you to be even more beautiful," Sax says as he crosses the room towards me. "Does it hurt too badly for you to..."

Sax never gets to finish the question as I meet him by the bed, our bodies crashing together as our lips find each other. I fumble at his belt as he gently stretches the waist of my underwear to clear my newly inked hip. "It'll be fine," I manage to gasp. "Just let me be on top."

I can feel Sax nod in agreement as I push him down to the bed, then jerk his jeans off and throw them to the floor. He pulls me on top of him, and together we make whatever lingering discomfort I may have had immediately fade away.

CHAPTER TWENTY-TWO

Sax

While Isobel is still sleeping, looking like the angel she is, I slip out of bed, get dressed and head outside to make a phone call. I never should have accepted her father's deal, but I didn't think I had a choice. Now, no matter the consequences to the Kings, I can't ask Isobel to give up her journey to help us when she only has a few years of an independent lifestyle left. The Kings can hire the best attorneys money can buy to try and get them out of the charges. And I...well, I'm ready to tell them the truth about everything, no matter the costs.

Finding her father's number in my phone, I press the button to call him and put the phone up to my ear.

"What?" he answers.

"How could you?" I grit out.

"Excuse me?" the governor asks in his holier than thou tone.

"How could you ask me to do this to Isobel when you *know* how important it is for her to live her life, her *limited* life the way she wants."

"So she told you about the Huntington's?" he asks as if it's a life choice and not a fatal disease.

"Yeah, she finally told me, so you and I are done. Do what you have to do, but I won't be a part of your plan any longer, you selfish fucking prick!"

"Then you better warn your friends to say goodbye to their families and get their finances in order before the feds put them away for life."

Squeezing my eyes shut at the pain this is going to cause them, I yell, "Fuck you!" before I end the call.

When I turn around to go back inside, Isobel is standing there on the back stoop in one of my t-shirts and nothing else, her arms wrapped around herself. The bottom of her new cherry blossom tattoo on her upper thigh sticks out, making her even sexier than before.

"Who were you talking to?" she asks softly, her voice still hoarse from sleep.

"No one," I answer automatically.

"You were yelling at them, so it must have been someone you know. What's going on?"

"Nothing, it's just club bullshit," I reply.

"Sax, please don't lie to me," she pleads, the look in her hazel eyes so sad it physically hurts my chest. "If it was no one, then let me see your phone," she says, holding out her palm for the device.

"Isobel," I start.

"Sax, just give me your phone."

"I can't," I tell her. "Listen, Iz, I-I hate lying to you."

"Then just tell me!" she snaps.

"Please promise me you'll hear me out," I beg. "Give me a chance to explain."

"Fine."

I'm not completely convinced, but I still begin to give her the truth. "Your father blackmailed me and the MC. He threatened to send us to prison for murder."

"Did you really do it? The murder?" she asks quietly.

"Yes, and he had evidence," I respond.

"God, Sax!" she exclaims, and I wait for her anger to rain down on me. Instead, she says, "I'm so, so sorry my dad did that. He really is such a dick. He's probably pissed because I lied and told him you and I were together."

"No, Iz, that's not it at all. You didn't do anything wrong," I assure her, because I see how guilty she feels and it's not fair for her to blame herself.

"Then why? Why would he blackmail you?" she asks.

"He blackmailed us, because...because he wanted me to convince you to stop running, to go back to nursing and make amends with him to, ah, help his reelection."

Her gasp of surprise and disbelief is so intense that I'm pretty sure she sucks all the air from *my* lungs.

"How..." she eventually asks. "How could you?"

"I'm done, okay?" I assure her. "I didn't know about the Huntington's or I never would have agreed! I told him I won't do it; I won't slow you down. I didn't know you were racing the clock! I just thought he was worried about the press seeing you on stage or drinking, th-that he was trying to control your life."

"Wow," she scoffs with a shake of her head before she starts to go back inside the house. I grab her arm to try and stop her.

"Let me go," she snaps.

"No. Never," I tell her honestly. "I'm falling in love with you, Isobel. So go wherever the hell you want. Just please, I'm begging you to let me come with you."

She shakes her head the whole time I'm talking while tears stream down her face.

"Please, Isobel," I beg. "Give me another chance."

She jerks away from me and storms back inside the house wordlessly. I follow behind, shutting our bedroom door while begging her not to leave without me. Despite my pleading, she never pauses as she gets dressed and throws her things back into her luggage.

"I'll do anything," I tell her. "*Anything* to make this up to you!"

Finally, she stops packing long enough to come up to me...and shoves her phone into my chest.

"Here!" she shouts, and the phone falls to the ground when she lets go. My hands feel numb, and I couldn't have caught it if I'd tried.

"What are you doing?" I ask. "I want you to sit down and talk to me, not give me your fucking phone!"

"Take it," she says. "There are photos on there, photos of the fake obituary and my mother's death certificate with her *actual* date of death. They should be enough to blackmail him right back. He would be ruined if the press figured out what he did. You can have them, just promise me that we're done. I *never* want to see you again."

"Isobel, no," I say as I reach for her face, but she steps backward.

"No, you don't get to touch me anymore!" she yells as she throws her purse on. "And if you try to follow me, I'll...I'll tell the MC everything you told me!" she threatens before she grabs up her luggage and guitar case and starts to the bedroom door.

"Please don't leave me. I love you!" I call out, and she pauses at the door for a second, her shoulders slumped. For one single moment, I think I may have gotten through to her. But then she yanks the door open, and War and Torin are on the other side.

"Everything okay in here?" Torin asks, looking between us.

"Get out of my way," she tells him before she shoulders past with her things. "Make sure he doesn't follow me!"

"Fuck!" I exclaim to the ceiling because I know I've lost her for good.

CHAPTER TWENTY-THREE

Isobel

M y head is so messed up that I have to pull over on the side of the road just a few miles from the house. I don't have the slightest idea what I'm doing or where I'm going.

Somehow that pisses me off more than Sax's betrayal.

Yes, I'm angry at him for lying to me and not telling me the truth about my father's blackmail from the beginning. But mostly I'm distraught because I had a plan. A good plan! One where I did whatever I wanted, when I wanted.

Now, I don't have the first clue how to pick back up and continue on my journey alone, the one I had once been so excited about.

Sax took that joy from me, and I want it back!

How the hell do I get it back?

Tears continue to stream down my face for several long minutes and I let them, hoping that, as soon as they dry up, things will be clearer.

I was wrong.

I may have stopped crying, but I still don't know what to do or where to go from here. I need a drink or ten to try to forget where I've been and who I've been with.

Then I remember the bar in Charlotte.

It's better than sitting in my car crying alone, so I plug in the address into my GPS and follow the robotic voice's step-by-step directions.

I still have three states to sing in, and North Carolina, my home state, is ironically one of them. Why haven't I done it before? I suppose I didn't want to chance being recognized as the governor's daughter.

Now though? I really don't give a shit. I hope someone sees me with my hair back to normal again and then my father is inconvenienced for a little while. It would serve him right, since he doesn't seem to mind screwing with my life.

SEVERAL HOURS and three drinks later, I'm feeling slightly better as I sing away my sorrows on stage.

Right up and until "I Hate Myself for Loving You."

God, the lyrics have never been truer than now.

I don't hate Sax for what he did. I hate myself for trusting him, for falling for his good looks and charm.

I can't even begin to find the strength to sing "Angel of the Morning" to the small lunch crowd, so I thank them for letting me vent my feelings through music and then leave the stage.

Maybe I need to get out of this state, out of the country.

I could still make it to the Balloon Fiesta if there's a flight...

But the idea of leaving just doesn't feel right. Not even the excitement of checking off an item on my bucket list makes me feel better. If anything, it feels empty, unlike before I met Sax when I felt euphoric.

I've never felt more alone than I do now, and it's all Sax's fault.

God, I wish I had never met him. Except, I don't wish that. Not really. Damn him and his ability to give me so many orgasms he short circuited my brain and made me fall for him!

I also hate the thought of Sax spending the rest of his life in prison because of my father. So what do I decide to do?

Maybe the stupidest thing ever.

I go home to ensure Sax and the Savage Kings won't suffer by my father's hand.

Not that I really have a home anymore, but I drive back to Raleigh all the same.

The mansion is locked when I get there, so I bang on the door until it opens. Even after almost four years, dear old dad never gave me a key, the jerk.

Imagine my surprise when he opens the door for me and not one of his minions.

"What did you want?" I ask him. "Me to dye my hair back? Done. Get back into nursing? I'll try. Go to town hall meetings with you? Fine, I'll do five and no more. And finally, I'm guessing you wanted some of mom's money." Pulling out a pen and my checkbook from my crossbody purse with shaking hands, I ask him, "How much? I'll write you a fucking check. But if I do this, you will *never* go after Sax or his friends again."

"Okay," he agrees, almost too easily as he blinks at me.

"Swear it to me. Swear it on mom's grave!" I yell at him.

"I-I swear."

My fingers tremble as I fill out all the little blanks on the check. And I get really pissed off when I even drop the damn pen. Twice. But I get it done eventually. Tearing the piece of paper free, I fold it in half and slip it into the front of his dress shirt pocket.

"I hate you more than words could ever express," I say truthfully before I turn to leave.

"Where are you going?" he calls out.

"Danny's," I answer. "You can send all messages and dates of appearances through him. I don't want to see or speak to you ever again."

CHAPTER TWENTY-FOUR

Sax

I haven't heard from Isobel since the day she left, but I didn't really expect to. She has every right to be pissed at me. What I did was the worst betrayal imaginable to her because it involved her father, who had lied to her about her mother and her own health. Still, I'm not going to give up.

First, I just need to take care of business with the Kings, and, if I'm still alive after I tell them the truth, I won't stop until I find Isobel, or I'm thrown in jail by the governor.

And while I have the photos Isobel gave me that cast the governor as a horrible human being who lied about his wife's death, I'm still not sure if it's enough to keep him from coming after the Kings. When I sent him screenshots of the photos from my phone, telling him I would send them to the media if he made a move against any of the Savage Kings, his only response was "We're good."

We're. Good.

I'm anything but fucking good, missing Isobel like hell these past few days, and hating myself for hurting her. But hopefully that means he's actually backing off. Still, I need to warn the guys, which is why I call a meeting as soon as Cooper is up for it. He didn't get the best news from the audiologist today, and we're still looking for who's responsible for the bombs.

"Any updates on suspects?" Torin asks Reece first, before the meeting begins.

"Actually, we just received one," the military man says solemnly. "This was spray painted in red on the side of the Savage Asylum last night. The sheriff deputy ran the artist off before they could finish. I was just waiting for Kira's parents to translate what was written for us."

"So it was in Russian. So we sure it's the Russians coming after us to get revenge?" Torin asks him.

"Looks like that's a safe bet." Reece's phone dings in front of him on the table. He picks it up and reads the screen before sharing it with us. "*The Savage Kings will all be poor dead peasants when I'm through with* – and that's all he had time to write."

"Wow," I mutter to myself as everyone else reacts.

"They said *I*, does that mean it's only one person?" Maddox speaks up and asks.

"That's a possibility," Reece agrees. "One angry Russian could be more dangerous than twenty, though, because it's easier for him to hide."

"Dammit," Torin grumbles. "How do we find him?"

"I'm running down close friends and family members of the men we killed. If I had to bet, I would put money on a close connection."

"Keep at it and let us know if you find out anything else," Torin says.

"Could someone please write all this shit down for me?" Cooper shouts, not only because his hearing is still fucked up but also because he's angry we're leaving him out.

"I've got it," Dalton says since he's sitting next to Coop. "Anyone got some paper and pen?" he asks, which of course reminds me of Isobel and her bucket list she always had close at hand.

"Ah, here," I say when I retrieve the tiny notepad and pen she gave me from my back pocket and toss it down in front of Dalton.

"Do you keep your deep dark secrets in here or what?" he asks. "Doodle Isobel's name in hearts, maybe?"

My glare tells him that I'm not in the mood to joke. But it does segue into the discussion we need to have now despite everything else we have going on.

"There's something all of you need to know, and it has to do with Isobel," I start. When I have their attention, I give them the cold hard truth. "The governor has a drone video from Escapades the night we killed the Russians. You can see us going in and coming out clearly enough to identify everyone at the table that was there."

"Holy shit," someone mutters, followed by more swears.

"It gets worse," I warn them. "The video also shows Ivan's guys throwing out the trash into a food truck. And Washington had the food truck followed all the way to the dump where they confiscated some of the bags of body parts."

Once I finish talking, the room is silent as they all try to digest just how fucked we are.

Eventually, Miles huffs and throws his hands up saying, "I knew it was too fucking easy!"

"But wait," Chase says as he rubs his fingers over his beard. "If the governor has this shit on us, why are we sitting here instead of in jail right now?"

"Because of Isobel," I say simply.

"She talked him out of it?" Torin asks.

"No, Lawrence, the governor, made me a deal. If I could rein in his wild child, convince her to go back to her old life and make amends with him so she could help his campaign, then he would leave us alone. He said we actually did him a favor by taking out the heroin trade trash."

"Is this what you and Isobel were yelling about?" War asks.

"Yes, I came clean with her right after I told her father that I'm done manipulating her for him."

"What the fuck?" Torin snaps. "How can you be done when that means we're all screwed?"

"Because she has a fatal genetic disease, the same disease that killed her mother when she was a kid. At best, she has ten good years left before she ends up in a wheelchair, unable to take care of herself. I can't make her give up on her bucket list to save our asses!"

"Shit. So what the hell are we going to do?" Abe asks.

"Hopefully the photos she gave me will be enough blackmail on the governor that he'll keep *his* blackmail to himself. I'm sorry. I think it's over, but I can't guarantee anything. He could come after us again, wanting something else. We need to face the fact that we're fucked."

"No fucking kidding," Torin grumbles.

"And, ah, there's something else I finally need to get off my chest," I tell them. "I've never really felt like I belonged with you, with the Savage Kings. When I first started prospecting way back when, I was actually working for the DEA. If I had learned anything about the Kings dealing hard drugs, I would've helped them take the MC down."

"Why the hell would you do that?" Torin asks as he and the other guys all glower at me.

"Because the girl I loved *died* in your bar from a drug overdose! I thought the Kings were dealing and were responsible. After I spent some time with you guys, I found out I was wrong. It was the Aryans."

"April Neil," Reece says.

"Yeah. How do you remember her name?" I ask him.

"Just do. A kid Chase knew brought her into the bar when she started seizing, but it was too late; she was gone. We made the one responsible pay."

"I know that now," I tell him. "I didn't until I started prospecting. I even tried to turn in my prospect cut to Deacon when I figured out the Kings weren't involved, but he wouldn't take it. He told me the MC needed me; 'a true north to guide the club in the right direction' or some silliness."

"Did you or Deacon know he was working for the DEA?" Chase asks Reece while pointing his finger at me.

"If he did, he never told me. This is the first I've heard of it," Reece responds.

"Well, now you all know the whole truth. I'm a fraud," I admit.

Slipping my arms out of my cut, I tell them, "I don't deserve to wear the Savage King patch and never have." Folding up the leather and placing it on the table, I look to Gabe and say, "I'll cover up the ink on my back as soon as Gabe can black it out; then you all can decide on my punishment."

"No," Torin grits out.

"No?" I repeat before understanding dawns on me. "No, I guess I don't need to bother covering up the ink. I'm a dead man, so no one will ever see it again. Do you even need to vote?" I ask.

"I meant no, don't cover up the tat because you're a Savage King as much as any of us. You've gone above and beyond everything we asked of you," Torin responds, which is the last thing I expected. "Not that I speak for everyone," he adds. "What say ye?"

"I second Torin," Chase says.

"I third," War responds.

"Anyone opposed to Sax keeping his patch and office?" Torin asks, and there's complete silence other than Dalton's scribbling in the tiny notepad.

"Then it's done."

"You're serious?" I say in disbelief.

"You never hurt the MC, did you?" Torin asks.

"No, I told the DEA I was wrong, that the drugs that killed April came from the Aryans."

"Then no harm, no foul," he replies. "And what you did with Isobel, to try and protect us all, that took guts, man. Whatever happens, we'll handle it, though, as a group."

"Wow, I don't know what to say," I mutter, my tongue feeling too thick to speak.

"Say you'll put your fucking cut back on," Chase tells me.

"Yeah, ah, okay," I reply before having to clear my throat. "I appreciate you all being so cool about all this, truly I do. But, um, I still may resign from my office and, ah, ask if I can transfer to the nomads."

"Why?" Abe asks.

"Isobel?" Chase asks.

"Yeah," I answer. "She's not going to settle down, and I don't want her to. I just want to go where she goes, before her time is up. That is, if she'll ever forgive me."

"All in favor of Saxon Cole transferring his membership to nomad if he so decides?" Torin asks.

"Yea," everyone says, and then Torin slams his gavel down. "Just say the word and I'll start the paperwork to assign you to the nomads, if you decide that's what you want. Even if you do, you'll always be a member of this charter, and we'll always have a seat for you at our table if you change your mind. Or if Isobel changes hers."

"Thanks, guys," I say, blinking back the moisture in my eyes. Even after all these years, I never felt like I belonged at the table with these men until now.

"Well," Chase starts. "I don't know about you, fuckers, but I need to see my woman. I say we cram in the van and haul ass down to South Carolina. No bikes; just us and our families."

"Agreed," Torin says along with the others.

"I think I'll take my chances out there and try to get my girl back," I tell them.

Dalton scribbles down our plans for Cooper, who sullenly says, "I need to find Jenna's kid. But you guys have fun. And good luck, man."

He offers me a fist bump across the table that I hit.

"You gonna be okay?" I ask.

"Yeah," he says. "I'm getting better at the lip reading. Although, I should probably get me one of those writing boards."

"Take care, and I'll check in with you when I'm back," I tell him, and he gives a nod of agreement.

I get the feeling he could use some time alone. And I'm probably going to have my hands full whenever I find out what country Isobel is currently charming.

CHAPTER TWENTY-FIVE

Isobel

"So, what's your plan now, Izzie?" Danny asks as we stand outside in his backyard while he grills the steaks we're having for dinner.

"I hate to do it because my father will believe it's all his idea, but I think I would like to try to get my license back. Is that just a crazy pipe dream?" I ask him.

"God, no," he says as he flips the steaks. "I can put in a good word for you with Doug Hannagan on the Board. And I know they would give it back to you if Lawrence asked…"

"No, I want to do it *without* his help," I say. "If I can't, then I'll try to be a CNA or something else in the medical field. I just want to help people. I miss it, you know?"

"Yeah, I thought you would eventually," he replies with a smile as he lays down the spatula to face me.

"I've been selfish trying to knock out my entire bucket list, only thinking about myself. I could do both, right?" I ask him. "I mean on vacations I could cross off bucket list items while still giving back."

"I'm really glad you came around to nursing again. That's where you belong, Izzie," Danny says before he leans over and kisses my cheek. When his lips cover mine, I immediately pull away.

"No, Danny. This...no," I tell him. "We're friends. That's all. I-I thought you knew that."

"We could try to be more. It could be amazing," he says.

"I love Sax," I blurt out without even thinking about it.

"Bullshit, you were just pretending you were with him to piss off your father. I know you, Izzie, better than anyone," he replies.

"Sax was working for my father, actually," I admit as I look down at my fidgeting, slightly trembling hands. "Not that I knew that at the time, but he was blackmailing him to manipulate me. Did you know?" I ask curiously since Daniel and my father are close.

"What? No, of course not! I would've told you if I did," he declares, and I actually believe him. He's never lied to me before.

"Well, it doesn't matter now anyway," I say with a heavy sigh. "Sax and I are over, and I caved. My father will get what he wanted and leave Sax alone."

"He was blackmailing him? Something serious?" Danny asks.

"Yeah?"

"What was it?"

"It doesn't matter now," I say again. I'll never tell anyone about the murder. "I took care of it." Despite what I know, I'm certain that Sax and the guys must have had a damn good reason to risk themselves like that. And I couldn't let those guys take the fall just because my father is a manipulative asshat.

"So you're back here because you love Sax and want to protect him?" Danny asks.

"Yeah, unfortunately. But also, I need more in my life to be happy, more than a selfish list of wants. I *want* to do something good, something worthwhile too. I realize that now."

"You're gonna get your license back, and then you can come work for me again," he says confidently. "The kids love you and so do I," he starts, and I know he's going to try and convince me that we could be more when I know in my heart Danny and I will only ever be friends.

"I'M NOT sure if working for you is a good idea, or if I should keep staying here with you," I tell him honestly. "I don't want to lead you on, and I really do wish I felt the same about you as I do about an outlaw."

"I wish you would stay, but I guess you're right. Maybe it is best," he agrees.

"Besides, I don't think I want to go back to working with kids. It's just too hard," I remark. "I'll figure out where to go next *if* the Board lets me."

God knows I could use the distraction of keeping myself busy with nursing if they reinstate me. Anything to take my mind off of Sax.

～

Sax

"WHERE'S ISOBEL?" I ask when I march right up to the governor's front door and wait impatiently for him to come talk to me.

"She's settling down, doing what I wanted her to do, thanks to you," he says.

"Wait. What the hell are you talking about?" I ask with my hands braced on my hips. I had assumed she was in Europe or some shit by now and I was going to be on the next flight there.

"She obviously cares about you and your gang since she was

willing to stick around and agreed to do a few events with me. She even gave me a few million for my campaign."

"Why would she do that?" I ask. "You're a dick."

"You really are dense," he says on an exhale. "I just told you! She cares about you and wants to protect you."

"She shouldn't," I tell him. "I have the photos she gave me to hold over your head."

"I should've known that she was behind those."

"Fuck your reelection. She's your daughter. Your *only* daughter! You need to let her go – let her live life while she still can on her own terms," I tell the jackass.

"I think Isobel has finally figured out what I've known all along – the only thing worth living for is protecting those you love. I tried to protect her mother from her illness; and when I of course failed, I tried to protect my daughter from witnessing her dreadful future. Watching Lily slip away a little more each day was agonizing."

"You saw her even after you threw her into the nursing home?" I ask.

"Every day," he responds. "Usually while Isobel was in school or with her friends or the nanny on the weekends. I couldn't resist seeing Lily even though it nearly killed me in the end when she couldn't speak to me or stop shaking. When she could talk, she told me to stop coming, to move on, find someone else, a 'real' mother for Isobel. She didn't understand that I couldn't ever love anyone else again."

"I'm sorry," I tell him truthfully. I can't imagine how hard it would be to lose the woman you love so slowly and painfully. "You did what you thought was best for Isobel, to help her have a normal life?"

"That's all I've ever wanted for her. I don't want to see her suffer, *ever*. Maybe one of your biker buddies can kill me once she has to be hospitalized."

"That can probably be arranged," I agree. "Besides, she won't need you there to take care of her then. That'll be my job. I hope."

"You're stubborn," he says. "Good. My daughter deserves nothing less, and she deserves better than the likes of you."

"I love her," I admit to him.

"You're a murderer."

"Not technically," I reply. "There's no blood on my hands directly, but I have stood by and watched them happen. I would do it again too."

"You don't have any regrets with the Russians?" he asks.

"No. They came after one of my brothers and were extorting money from his in-laws. They had to be dealt with."

Narrowing his eyes at me, he says, "I'll make you a deal. If any more trash needs to be taken out, you'll be my garbage men."

"As long as they deserve it, we could probably help," I agree. "The guys would have to vote on it to approve it."

"Then I give you permission to date my daughter. If that's what she wants," he agrees.

"I didn't need your permission, but I guess it will make things easier," I respond. "Now, tell me where she is. How do I find her?"

"The last time I saw her, Isobel told me she was going to Danny's," he says, which drives the knife in my heart a little deeper.

"What's his address?" I ask on a sigh, because I don't care if she's sleeping with him or not, I still want to be with her, if she can forgive me. In fact, I deserve every second of the pain.

CHAPTER TWENTY-SIX

Sax

"I need to talk to Isobel," I tell the asshole through clenched teeth when he comes into his office wearing goofy-ass scrubs with cars or some shit on them. Her father gave me his home address, but it was a weekday, and no one was there. Or, if Isobel was there, she didn't answer the door. So, I decided to pay the good doctor a personal visit at work instead.

"She's no longer staying with me," he says.

Grabbing his throat, I pin him to the wall. "If you're lying to me, I'll kill you."

"She's not," Danny squeaks.

"Where can I find her?" I ask, releasing my grip on his throat.

"She said she was getting her own place, but I don't know the address," he says while rubbing the sides of his neck, which is disappointing. "But right now I know where she's at. She's meeting with the Board to try and get her nursing license back."

"Seriously?" I ask. "She wants to go back into nursing? Why isn't she traveling the world or whatever?"

"She said she realized she missed helping others. Guess traveling on her own wasn't fun anymore."

"I don't understand..."

"She loves you."

"She loves me? She said that?" I ask.

"Unfortunately," he mutters. "So, you better fix things with her. Look, I'm not going to lie to you. I love Isobel, and I've told her as much."

Seeing my face darken in anger, he holds up his hands in surrender before I explode. "We grew up together; we've worked together. She sees me like a brother. I respect that, and I'm not like her father. I'm not going to push something on her that she doesn't want."

I sink down into one of the nearby chairs while Danny makes this confession, my anger slowly fading away. "I'm sorry," I tell him. "I had this idea in my head that you were a vulture, circling the carcass of our relationship just waiting to swoop down for a feast. After meeting her father and seeing how much he liked you, it just never occurred to me that you might actually be a good friend to her."

"Don't feel bad," Danny snorts as he moves around his desk. He sits down and pulls a notepad out of a drawer to begin to scribble down some notes. "I haven't held you in the highest esteem either, you know. You looked like a drunken fling, or even worse, just a tool to infuriate her father. She's talked a lot about you since she's been back, though, and now I know that none of that is true. You make her happy, and that's enough for me. Here," he adds, tearing a piece of paper off the notepad and sliding it across his desk. "This is the address of the health department where the nursing licensing board is located. She's supposed to be meeting them at two o'clock."

"Thanks, man," I sigh as I get to my feet. "What do you say we start over the next time we run into each other and put all this behind us?" I ask him as I pick up the paper from the desk and slip it into my cut.

"You treat Isobel well, and you and I will never have a problem," Danny says. Getting to his feet, he walks to his office door, holding it open for me in invitation. "Go take care of her, Sax. I'll send her a message later to ask her how things went with the Board, and make sure she knows you're in town."

I give him a nod and then leave the office. I have to suppress the urge to break into a jog and force myself to walk calmly to my bike outside, even though it feels like anxiety is crushing my heart. Even if she loves me, can she ever forgive me for the betrayal her father forced on us?

Before I crank up my bike, I run the address Danny gave me through my personal phone, glancing at the directions on my app. The health department is only a few blocks away, so I recite the street names in my head to settle my nerves as I roar through town. It's not even one o'clock yet when I pull into the huge parking lot leading to the three-story stone building that houses the health department, but I still cruise through each aisle of the lot, looking for Isobel's white Lexus.

When I don't immediately spot her car, I rumble up to the front entrance of the building and find a place to park my bike. I notice while I'm taking off my helmet that almost a dozen people are outside staring at me after my tour of the parking lot, and there are even faces in the windows glaring down at me. Before I kill the engine on my Harley, I twist the throttle while I'm sitting in neutral, the roar from my custom-made straight pipes damned near rattling the glass in the cars surrounding me.

With a grin and a wave to everyone watching, I kill the engine and then walk up to the main entrance, prepared to stake it out the rest of the day, if necessary. Fortunately, after only half an hour of watching people come and go, I spot a pristine, white Lexus pulling into the lot. It's only one-thirty, so I'm hopeful she'll have time to talk to me before she has to rush inside. I go stand right in the middle of the walkway, making sure that I don't catch her by surprise.

Unfortunately, despite my attempts to make myself obvious, Isobel approaches me while looking down at a folder in her hands and doesn't acknowledge my presence until she almost bumps into me. Raising her eyes briefly, she mutters, "Excuse me," before starting to step around me.

"Isobel," I call her name softly, bringing her to an abrupt halt. She slowly turns towards me, closing the folder and squaring her shoulders as her gaze rises to mine.

"Sax," she exhales my name in a whisper. "What are you...how did you know I was here?"

"I had to come for you," I shrug. "I talked to your dad and then to Danny over at his office. They resisted a little at first, but they both eventually gave me their blessing and told me I could find you here."

"They gave you their blessing?" Isobel scoffs. "What does that even mean, Sax? What did you think was going to happen if you came here? That I'd swoon over your grand gesture and forgive you for what happened? That I'd run off back to the coast with you and be your...what did your friends call it, your 'old lady'?"

"No, Isobel, please, it's not like that," I protest. I can feel people stopping to stare at the two of us, but I press on, not caring who hears me or what they think. "When I drove up here, I couldn't even think. I had no idea what I was going to do or say. I only knew that I couldn't breathe, I couldn't rest, I couldn't do anything without seeing you again. I went to your dad's house, because it was the only place I knew to start. I was prepared to beat him half to death to find out where you were, and for what he had done to you...to us," I pause for breath and see the faintest hint of a smile flash on Isobel's lips.

"I told him that I knew about your Huntington's, and about what he had done to your mother. He told me some things, things that he needs to talk to you about himself; but ultimately, I told him...I told him I want to be yours, Izzie. I want to be the person you can rely on, the person who stands by you all the days of your life and helps you through whatever comes. I want him to keep all his bullshit to himself, and just let you and I have a real chance. That's what he gave his blessing to."

"Do you really think my father's blessing is the kind of ringing endorsement that's going to impress me?" Isobel teases me, the small smile still playing around her lips. Her eyes narrow and her face turns stern as she continues, "Besides, Sax, what are you even hoping for? That I'll run off with you, hop on your boat and sail into the sunset? I'm done running. I'm going to try and get my nursing license back. I'm going to use the time I have left to try to help people, to give something back."

"What made you change your mind?" I ask her, at a loss for anything else to say.

"A lot of things. Like helping Cooper, having someone depend on me. How is he doing, anyway?"

"He's fine," I start to defer with a wave of my hand, but abruptly stop myself with a sigh. "He's not fine. I just didn't want to change the subject," I admit. "He's still deaf, and he's hell-bent on finding that girl Jenna's family, especially her child. He feels personally responsible for what happened, and it's tearing him apart."

"I understand the feeling," Isobel says. "That's another reason I want to get back to doing something that matters, rather than just follow my own selfish whims. What my father did to you, to your friends, that was at least partly on me and the decisions I'd made. I've tried to make that right, at least."

"If that's what you really want, you know I'll support you all the way," I tell her as I move a step closer. She doesn't withdraw, so I tentatively reach out my hand and lay it on her arm. "I want to be here for you, whatever you decide, and wherever life takes you."

"Sax..." Isobel breathes deeply, then blinks up at me, obviously fighting back tears. "I want to believe you, but how would you even make that work? You've got your family, the Savage Kings. You've got some crazy bomb-terrorist after you, and you said the jobs you do keep you out on your boat most of the time. They need you, and I don't want to rip you away from your life."

"I want you to be my life," I tell her, without even thinking of how cheesy I must sound. "I mean it. Look," I add, turning my back to her so she can see my cut.

"I mean, it's a nice ass, Sax, but I'm not sure...oh, your patches are different!" Isobel realizes. "You changed the bottom one. Why does it say Nomad? Does that mean something in biker lingo?"

I let out a mirthless laugh as I turn back to face her. "Yeah, I suppose it means I'm unemployed." When Isobel just stares at me unblinking, I try to explain it in a bit more detail. "It means I'm still a member of the club, but I've resigned from my official charter, my 'group' down at Emerald Isle. I can work for any charter, but I only get paid by the job, not a percentage of the earnings. It means I'm free to go wherever I want to go and do whatever I want to do. It means nothing is holding me back from following you anywhere, everywhere, for as long as you will let me."

Isobel stares at me in silence before suddenly shivering, breaking our eye contact. "I have to get inside for my interview," she says as she turns away.

"Isobel, please!" I call, starting to follow her into the building.

"If you really mean it," she says over her shoulder as she opens the door to the health department. "Then stay here while I talk to the Board. Once I'm done...if you're going to follow me anyway, I suppose I should show you the hotel I'm staying at until I get an apartment lined up."

"I'll be here," I promise her as I steal a quick kiss that she deepens, telling me that I'm actually making some progress. When I finally make myself pull away because I know she has to get to her appointment, I tell her, "As long as you'll have me, I'll always be here."

EPILOGUE

Sax

Six months later...

As soon as I get off the elevator on the pediatric floor of the hospital, I can hear Isobel strumming a tune on her guitar. I follow the melody down the hall past the nurses' station, pausing for a moment to hide the present I brought for her before heading down to the community room. The entire area is decorated with strings of colored lights and tinsel, hiding the normally sterile walls of the hospital and filling the floor with Christmas cheer.

When I walk in the room, a dozen children are gathered around the love of my life sitting by a small tree. Her hair is back to the same turquoise and purple it was when we met, which I love, although she enjoys changing it to various bright colors every few weeks to surprise the kids.

"All right, everyone," Isobel tells the children when she spots me and puts her guitar back into its case. "It's almost time for me to go, so I need all of my good little boys and girls to head back to their rooms!"

A chorus of good-natured groans greet her announcement, but the children all stand and begin to file out past me. "Hi, Sax!" a few greet me from behind the surgical masks they're wearing. I bend down and scoop up one of the tiny forms, five-year-old Sara, who begins giggling immediately.

"No tickles, Sax!" she manages to squeak out before I place a kiss on top of the pink and white scarf she wears to keep her scalp warm. I put her down, and still giggling, she races off down the hall.

"No tickles for me either, please," Isobel grins as she picks up her guitar case and comes over to me. "I will take the kiss, though," she adds, leaning up to brush lips with me. "I need to put in some notes, and then I'll be ready to go!"

"There's no rush. I've got your car all packed up," I tell her. Over the two-week Christmas break we're going on a cruise to the Lofoten Islands of Norway to see the Northern Lights, another item to check off of her bucket list. "We just have to go pick up Willy at the apartment, and then we can head out."

"You didn't bring her with you?" Isobel asks.

"Hell no," I begin, before a friendly scowl from Isobel reminds me to watch my language around the kids. "You know I can't get that hairy fiend into the carrier without you!"

With a laugh, Isobel sits down at the computer terminal. "I still don't understand how your cat can be so difficult for you to handle. She's an absolute sweetheart when I pick her up."

"You've seen yourself what happens when I try!" I protest. "She's not 'my' cat. She just started hanging around my boat because I would leave food out for her, and one day I woke up with her sleeping on me! I don't think I've had a peaceful night since she decided I was her favorite pillow."

"I didn't know how bad it was until we brought her up here," Isobel grins. "She is pushy about bedtime, if you and I spend too much time...ahem," she clears her throat as she looks around the nurses' station at her co-workers. "Well, you can tell she's the jealous type."

Another nurse sits down beside Isobel with a chart, then glances over at the two of us. "Hey, guys, how are things going?" she asks us. "You still enjoying peds, Izzie?"

"I love it," Isobel gushes to her co-worker. "I mean, in a lot of ways, this has been the most heartbreaking, devastating place I've ever worked. But seeing these kids fight, their bravery and their triumphs...it's hard to explain, but I love it here."

"You were born for this," the nurse says to her. "There are days that will almost break you, but you're right, it's all about the triumphs. You always keep that in mind, and you'll be fine. Enjoy your vacation, you two!" she adds as she gets up and walks down the hall.

"These kids help you as much as you help them, don't they?" I ask her.

"They do," Isobel agrees. "Seeing how they have to fight when they're so young, how well they handle everything, it really gives me perspective, you know? It makes me realize just how blessed I am to have these good years."

"Oh, there's going to be a lot of good years," I reassure her. "Hey, before we leave, do you think we can get the kids back together for a few minutes? I wanted to get here a little earlier, and hear you play."

"Sax, you know shift change is busy..." Isobel begins to protest, trailing off as she sees another one of her co-workers leading the children back into the community room. "Marie, are you doing something with the kids?" Isobel asks the nurse.

"Your man there called a little earlier and asked us if we could get them together for a few songs out here in the lobby," Marie replies, shaking a finger at me. "He said he had a surprise for you!"

"Sax, what are you up to?" Isobel turns to me to ask as I reach behind the filing cabinet to produce the present I hid earlier.

"Ta-Da!" I grin as I show her the guitar case I brought in with me. "I bought you something."

Isobel looks down at her own guitar case, then stares at me in shock. "You bought me a guitar? Sax, that's crazy, you know how much I love mine!"

"I suppose I should say I bought 'us' a present, then. I bought a guitar so that you can teach me to play. I know how much you worry about your hands, and what may happen one day if, you know..."

"You want me to teach you to play, so if my tremors get too bad, you can do it for me," she whispers.

"You'll be able to sing," I tell her as I reach down to give her a one-armed hug. "And I can be your hands. I'll sing along, of course, as long as it doesn't scare the kids."

"You will not," she laughs. "You've got gravel in your throat, I swear."

"Will you do it, though?" I ask her. "Teach me, let me be a part of your music?"

"Of course I will," Isobel says as she leans up to kiss my cheek. "It will take a long time for you to be as good as me, but..."

"We've got time, baby," I reassure her. "I'll be with you every step of the way. Come on, let's show it to the kids, and maybe we can pick out a simple song together."

"Okay," she agrees as she picks up her own guitar. "Let's take a look at this thing and see if you got ripped off or not," she laughs as she walks into the lobby and sits down inside the circle of children. I linger behind for a moment, surreptitiously sending a text from my phone, before I walk in and sit down beside her, laying my guitar case down in front of her.

"Open it up and take a look," I tell her.

Isobel leans over to flip open the clasps on the new guitar case.

When she opens it up; however, her body freezes before she slowly raises her hand, holding the small box that I had placed inside the case.

"Open it up and take a look," I repeat with a smile, as the children gasp and some begin to clap.

Isobel opens the jewelry box to reveal the sparkling princess cut diamond ring I had made especially for her. Before she can say anything, I move to squat on one knee in front of her. "I wanted to bring it upstairs and do this with all of your friends," I tell her as I turn to wink at the children gathered around us. "Isobel Washington, meeting you has been the greatest joy in my life. The only thing that could surpass it would be living with you forever as my wife. Will you marry me?"

Isobel's cheeks had taken on a flaming blush as she had gazed at the ring, and when she reaches over to throw her arms around my neck, I can barely hear her "Yes!" over the cheers of the children.

"Yes, yes," she laughs as she kisses me and then lets me go so that I can take the ring and slip it on her finger. When I abruptly stand up, she asks, "Wait, where are you going?"

"I've got one more surprise for you and all of our best buddies," I tell her as I spread my arms towards all the children. "I'm not sure, but I think I heard some great big reindeer rumble up outside!"

I had timed it almost perfectly, and a moment later the clomp of heavy boots filled the hall, where the nurses had all gathered. A burly, red-suited figure that I recognized as my brother, War, stomps into the lobby, gently dropping a huge bag onto the floor.

"HO-HO-HO!" War bellows with his hands on his hips, while the rest of the Savage Kings from Emerald Isle gather in the hall behind him. They smile and wave as the kids leap to their feet, rushing to gather around the giant Santa biker.

"Tone it down, there, Santa," I call to War. "Don't worry, kids, I talked to him and I made sure he brought everything you guys wished for!"

Turning back to Isobel, I offer her a hand and pull her to her feet.

"Merry Christmas, baby!" I tell her as I wrap her in my arms and kiss her.

"Sax, this...this is the best gift you could have possibly given me. Thank you, thank you so much!" Isobel says as she squeezes me close.

"Did I forget to tell you?" I ask innocently. "The Savage Kings do a toy drive every year. War especially looks forward to it. He would wear that Santa suit everywhere if he could."

"But to do it for our kids here, and have your crew come all this way..." Isobel says before I stop her with another kiss.

"When I told the guys about the work you're doing, and about these kids, they couldn't wait to get here. The truth is, I love them almost as much as you do. I'm glad you decided to come here. I'm glad I get to be here. Things like this really make life worthwhile."

"People like you make this life worthwhile," Isobel corrects me. "I can't wait to spend mine with you, Saxon Cole."

"Well, soon-to-be Mrs. Isobel Cole, let's help our little buddies open their presents, and then you and I can head out. I've added a few things to my little notebook that I can't wait to show you."

"You're still working on your bucket list?" she asks me in surprise.

"No, baby, this is no bucket list. This is my Isobel list, filled with things I can only do with you. To you. For now, though, I can't wait to introduce everyone to my fiancée."

The End

ABOUT THE AUTHORS

New York Times bestselling author Lane Hart and husband D.B. West were both born and raised in North Carolina. They still live in the south with their two daughters and enjoy spending the summers on the beach and watching football in the fall.

Connect with D.B.:
Twitter: https://twitter.com/AuthorDBWest
Facebook: https://www.facebook.com/authordbwest/
Website: http://www.dbwestbooks.com
Email: dbwestauthor@outlook.com

Connect with Lane:
Twitter: https://twitter.com/WritingfromHart
Facebook: http://www.facebook.com/lanehartbooks
Instagram: https://www.instagram.com/authorlanehart/
Website: http://www.lanehartbooks.com
Email: lane.hart@hotmail.com

Join Lane's Facebook group to read books before they're released, help choose covers, character names, and titles of books! https://www.facebook.com/groups/bookboyfriendswanted/

Find all of Lane's books on her Amazon author page!

Sign up for Lane and DB's newsletter to get updates on new releases and freebies!